MATCH MADE ONLINE

SARAH THAM

First Edition

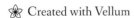 Created with Vellum

To Arthur—I love you!

PROLOGUE

My white blouse was neatly buttoned up to my neck and my navy-blue skirt covered my ankles, as was deemed modest attire for a 12-year-old girl. Like a row of duck- lings, my four siblings and I followed my parents through the entrance of a large conference center, and my eyes widened as we joined the mass of thousands of other fami- lies bustling around. Pride swelled in my chest, and I held my head high knowing that we were not just average, run- of-the-mill Christians. We were members of the Institute— an elite, ultra-conservative, nation-wide homeschooling program. And we had gathered together for this annual conference to learn how to better live out the rules and principles handed down from our esteemed leader who seemed to have direct revelation from God regarding all matters of life.

The breakout session for young ladies was about to begin, and I eagerly found a seat near the front of the meeting room. Microphone in hand, a woman in her 20s took the stage and welcomed us with an enthusiastic, "Hello girls!" She held up a large, red paper heart. "This represents your heart. Let's see what happens to your heart when you start dating."

I leaned forward, riveted. Dating was rarely talked about in the Institute. All the usual sources of information about this subject—TV shows, movies, and pop music—were banned, so this was my chance to gain some valuable information.

"Every time you date and get attached physically or emotionally to someone, you give away a piece of your heart to that person," the speaker explained. A few gasps were heard as she ripped the paper heart into pieces and handed them to random audience members. "After all your years of dating and heartbreak, what will happen?" She held up one tiny scrap for all to see. "You'll have barely anything left to give to your future husband."

A hush fell across the room as the object lesson sunk in.

"We've all seen those *other* girls. They don't guard their hearts and they're miserable. They date, they break up, they cry, and then they eat a gallon of ice cream." She mimed scooping dessert into her mouth which sent the crowd into giggles.

"There's a better way called courtship. Wait for a godly, young man to ask your father for permission to court you. Go on chaperoned outings and let your parents guide the process. Your parents are your authorities, just like an umbrella over you. As long as you stay under their umbrella of protection, Satan can't attack you."

My cheeks suddenly reddened and I sank down in my seat, wishing I could disappear. Although I was too young to date, I had already started developing crushes on cute boys from my church and neighborhood. I was ashamed to admit how often I daydreamed about them. Had I already lost some pieces of my heart? My ever-constant companion, Fear, stealthily coiled around me like a boa constrictor, and hissed in my ear, "Better shut down those romantic feelings and be more careful to guard your heart!"

From that day forward, I was determined to stay vigilant when it came to the dangerous realm of romance.

WINTER

ONE
ONLINE DATING
13 YEARS LATER

"I'm going to quit online dating!" I emphatically set down my chai tea latte, making it slosh. Holiday music jingled over the speakers, reminding me that I would spend another Christmas single, and that was probably for the best.

Sitting across the cafe table was my long-time friend, Zia. She wore a burgundy sweater, and I noticed that her dark brown skin perfectly matched the color of her coffee. She peered curiously at me over the rim of her glasses. "Why? You just started a month ago, for goodness' sake!"

"Well, none of the guys seem right for me." I let out a sigh. "Can you believe there was a 50-year-old guy who kept messaging me? That's twice my age!"

"Ew, that's messed up!" Zia wrinkled her nose at the thought.

The frustration of the past month bubbled up to fuel my rant. "You should see the bad pictures men post on their profiles! Who wants to see a guy's shirtless bathroom mirror selfie? Or a guy proudly posing with his skate-board? Or they just leave their profile completely blank!" I raked my hands through my thick black hair. "At least the decent photos show men mountain biking, wakeboarding, and snowboarding. But you know I'm not into that stuff at all. I don't do many activities that end in 'ing.'"

"Except 'teaching'." Zia winked at me. "That's one activity that takes up your entire life."

"Exactly! I barely have time for anything else, including dating. That's why I'm quitting."

Zia didn't look convinced. "Excuse me, how many dates have you even gone on?"

"One," I mumbled.

"One this week?"

I rolled my eyes. "One in my *entire life*. And it wasn't even good." I cringed as I remembered my first date. My mind flashed back to three weeks ago. There I was, on my first date, nervously waiting at a restaurant and my would-be prince charming had shown up late, looked nothing like his photos, and spent the evening discussing his conspiracy theories.

"So you've gone on one bad date, and now you want to quit. Don't you think you need to put in a little more effort?"

"I just wish a guy would show up at my door and ask me out. It feels weird to have to put myself out there. Aren't women supposed to let the guys pursue them?" I thought back to the teaching about courtship which had been held up as the ultimate path toward marriage.

"Sarah, Sarah." Zia's tight curls bounced as she shook

her head in exasperation. "There's nothing wrong with being proactive. You need to start thinking about your future. I don't want you to wait too long and miss out. I didn't get married until my mid-30s and dating is even more difficult the older you get, let me tell you!"

"It's just so overwhelming."

"Listen, I want you to go home and make a profile on LoveLinkup. It's the best dating site out there. That's where I met Steven." She flashed her wedding ring at me.

"But LoveLinkup is so expensive!"

"You can start by making a free profile."

I opened my mouth to protest, but I had no excuses left.

"Hey," Zia's tone softened. "I believe that God has a good plan for your life. But He might not just drop a husband into your lap. He might want to teach you something through the process of dating. Let's pray about it." With that, she reached across the table, grasped my hands, and began to pray for me and for my future husband, whoever he may be. Her words filled my soul with fresh encouragement and I resolved to try one more time.

HOME. I loved being home, nestled in familiarity. Hot cocoa in hand, I paused to breathe in the pine scent from our Christmas tree and admire the twinkling lights. Every evening after work, I hung out with my parents and siblings as we binged-watched TV shows, worked on jigsaw puzzles, or just sat around talking. Some might call it a sheltered life, but I loved my cozy cocoon. Besides, it came with the perks of cheap rent, free Wi-Fi, and home cooked dinners every night. Why would I ever want to leave?

However, Zia's challenge to start thinking about my future had lit a fire under me. Home, as I knew it, would one day change. My parents would age and my siblings would eventually fly the nest, one after the other. I needed to start looking for a new home, and start building a family unit of my own. If only I could skip the awkward dating step.

I stretched out in front of the fireplace and cracked open the lid of my laptop. It was time to shake off my apathy and get moving.

"Whatcha doing?" My younger sister, Rebekah, curled up next to me.

"Just checking LoveLinkup. Want to see?" A few days ago, I set up my dating profile and had filled out a long questionnaire that would supposedly help the system match me with someone compatible. I'd even uploaded a cute photo of myself standing in a garden, showing off my big smile, tan skin, and dark brown hair and eyes.

"You have matches!" Rebekah squealed, as only a teenage girl could, and scooted closer.

A list of names and profiles appeared on the screen. But unfortunately, the photos were blurred out since I was only using the free version. I chewed my lip as I surveyed these mystery men. "Look at this guy—Arthur. He sent me a message. His bio says he's 'passionate about Jesus, family, friends, and community.' He must be pretty serious about his faith if he mentioned Jesus."

"It says he's 33. That's 8 years older than you. Are you ok with that?"

"At least he'll be more mature. I don't really want to date a young guy that's still riding around on a skateboard or anything like that. As long as he doesn't look too old."

"Can you reply to him?" Rebekah squinted at my screen. "And what does he *look* like?"

"I have to sign up for a subscription first." I sighed. "But it costs over $100. I could buy some nice boots with that money instead!"

"Sarah!" Rebekah poked me in the side. "You're always careful with money. Stop being so frugal for once! Just do it!"

"Alright, here we go." It was time to get into the game and start taking action. I whipped out my credit card and entered my information. Within a few minutes, my subscription was activated. We leaned forward breathlessly as Arthur's profile photo came into view.

"Huh," was all I could say.

The grainy headshot didn't have much of a wow factor. All I could tell was that he appeared to be Chinese. I took a sip of my hot cocoa. "Let's check if he has more photos. Hopefully they're good."

In the first photo, Arthur stood in the distance. His face was deadpan, and his eyes were hidden by sunglasses. He wore shapeless, olive-green pants, and a rumpled gray shirt. Whoever had taken the photo had accidentally covered a corner of the frame with their thumb.

I swallowed nervously. "Ok, not the best. Next photo."

This time, Arthur appeared to be on the Great Wall of China, but his brow was furrowed together and his eyes squinted.

Rebekah grimaced. "Yikes, he looks angry."

"I think he just has sun in his eyes. Hmm. Next photo."

This time, Rebekah started laughing. "I'm not sure which is worse: his baggy dad jeans or his bright green windbreaker straight from the '90s!"

"Arg! These photos are terrible!" I covered my face with both hands. "I just wasted my money on this guy."

"Wait, we have to see the last photo!" Rebekah giggled, clearly having too much fun with this.

I reluctantly clicked on it, bracing myself for more disappointment. But to my surprise, a well-framed, close-up of Arthur's smiling face appeared. The caption read "Central Park, New York." He wore a blue jacket, and he was leaning against a bridge with misty green trees in the background. His straight black hair was clipped in a simple buzz cut, and his face was clean-shaven. He wore no sunglasses, so I could see his soft brown eyes, feathered by a few wrinkles at the corners. There was kindness in them. I lingered. His smile was gentle and friendly. He wasn't movie-star handsome, but something about him reminded me of my cup of hot cocoa: inviting, warm, and sweet.

"Well now," I whispered, my voice unexpectedly hoarse. "This photo isn't too bad. Maybe I'll give this Arthur guy a try."

ARTHUR and I exchanged a few messages, and everything seemed to be getting off to a good start. But later that night as I tried to sleep, Fear slithered into my mind and I heard the old, familiar hiss of doubt, "You don't know the first thing about dating. You're too shy and reserved. Once things get serious, you'll get cold feet and break up. Why drag this poor man into an inevitable romantic disaster?"

Yes, Arthur would be better off with someone else. He didn't deserve to contend with all of my issues. I should just forget this whole fantasy and try to enjoy my life as a single person. So I did what seemed most logical—I called up customer service and asked them to close my account and refund my money. I was still within the refund period, after all.

Remembering my manners, I dashed off a brief message to Arthur to end things gracefully. It would be rude to just disappear. As an afterthought, I included my full name and said that he was free to look me up on social media, not thinking that he actually would. And that was that.

Or so I thought.

TWO
FIRST DATE

Take deep breaths. My shaking hands clutched the steering wheel as I drove out of the school parking lot. After a long day with students, I looked a little disheveled, and my sensible jeans and blouse that buttoned up to my neck didn't exactly scream first date outfit. But at least I was *going* on a date which was a minor miracle given my attempt to quit online dating. Again.

After snagging a parking spot at a nearby coffee shop, I silently sent up a prayer. *God, please don't let him be too old or scary.* Then I exited my car, marched up to the heavy, glass door and courageously swung it open. Having arrived early, I looked around for a spot to wait, only to realize with a start that my date was already inside! Our eyes locked, and I saw Arthur Tham face to face for the first time.

"Hi, I'm Arthur."

"Hi, I'm Sarah." I shook his hand and was surprised by

its warmth and softness. My cold, shaking hand momentarily relaxed in his.

"May I order you something to drink?" Arthur motioned to the counter.

I stepped closer to him as we looked at the menu, side by side. I caught a whiff of something spicy with a hint of sweetness, like cinnamon. But it wasn't coming from the coffee—it was Arthur. I didn't usually get close enough to any men to actually smell them. *My, that's a pleasant scent!*

I tried to regain my focus. "I'm not much of a coffee drinker. I'll just get a chai tea latte."

"What a coincidence. I don't drink coffee either," Arthur remarked. He ordered a strawberry smoothie and paid for both of our drinks.

We settled at a small table next to a large window. The afternoon light was beginning to fade, and a red sunset lit up the heavens. I took a moment to study Arthur's appearance, and thankfully, there was nothing scary about him. He was medium height, dressed in jeans and a gray polo shirt, and his boyish smile made him seem younger than his age.

"I was surprised when you closed your dating account," Arthur said. "But I'm glad you left your name, so I was able to find you on social media."

"Yeah, I kind of got cold feet. But thanks for reaching out and inviting me to coffee. I'm an English teacher and I noticed your message was well written and had perfect grammar, so I felt like I should at least give you a chance."

"Well, I'm glad to hear that!" Arthur chuckled and relaxed back in his chair.

I took a sip of tea and tried to think of a good topic to kick off our conversation. "So, do you like to read?" I cringed a little when I realized I was reverting into teacher mode, but Arthur didn't seem to mind the question at all.

"Yes, I do! Especially books about dating and marriage. That's a topic that really interests me. Have you read any relationship books?"

"Um, well...." I racked my brain. "When I was a teen, I read *I Kissed Dating Goodbye* by Joshua Harris."

"I actually don't like that book." He spoke with conviction and passion which caught me off-guard.

"Why? I thought it was great."

"I think it generated a lot of fear around dating and contributed to many people getting married later in life or not getting married at all."

"Tell me more." I leaned forward on the table, curiosity piqued by this man who had strong opinions.

"Well, I've dated a lot of women who were taught that they need to be passive when it comes to dating. They think they need to wait around to be pursued. But it doesn't always work out that way."

Passive. Little did he know that he was describing my own experience. "Well, what do you recommend then, when it comes to dating?"

"I believe it's really a numbers game."

"A numbers game?" I raised my eyebrows. "What does that mean?"

"That means that the more people you meet and date,

the more likely you are to find a spouse. It takes a while to find the right person to marry because so many things have to line up on both sides. I've been dating for several years now, and I've already gone on 60 to 80 first dates." He paused to casually sip his smoothie.

All the noise in the coffee shop seemed to fade into the background as I tried to process what he had just told me. *A numbers game. That actually sounds pretty logical. But 60 to 80 first dates? That's wild!* I finally found my voice. "That's an interesting perspective. But it's very opposite of how I was raised."

Arthur cocked his head to the side. "How were you raised?"

"I grew up in a tight-knit Christian family. When I was 6 years old, we joined a special homeschool group that was...a little strange."

"How so?"

As I contemplated my answer, I shifted my gaze out the window towards the twilight sky. I usually kept my childhood experiences hidden away, and didn't talk about them with anyone, let alone with strangers. But Arthur seemed genuinely interested, and something about his candor inspired me to open up as well.

"Unfortunately, it turned out to be a cult. We weren't locked up in some building or forced to do anything against our will, but sometimes mental handcuffs are the strongest."

"That sounds very difficult," Arthur said softly with compassion in his eyes. "What were you taught about dating?"

Without much effort, past memories rushed forward to the forefront of my mind. "I was taught that dating was like giving away pieces of my heart."

"Yikes! Then you must think that I have pieces of my heart strewn all over the place!"

Arthur laughed at himself, and I couldn't help but laugh aloud, too. A deep, healing laugh.

"In my case," Arthur's tone turned thoughtful, "dating multiple people has refined my character and helped me figure out what I'm really looking for in a spouse. I wouldn't be who I am today without all of those experiences."

"I've never thought about it that way. I'm just getting started with dating, so I have a lot to learn."

"I'm still learning, too."

His warm, understanding smile sent a small tingle down my spine.

Our conversation continued to flow back and forth like a game of ping pong between two perfectly matched players. More than once did Arthur succeed at making me laugh, and I found myself growing more comfortable around him with each passing minute. Before long, the sky had turned black and I reluctantly realized that I should head home.

As we wrapped up our conversation, Arthur smoothly made a pitch for a second date. "Have you ever been to Woodland Park? I'd love to take you there for our next date."

I was flattered by his intentionality, but a worrisome thought flitted through my mind. *Arthur seems like a great guy, but why is he still single even after dating dozens of women? What if there's something wrong with him? Maybe I should end things now.*

But I didn't want things to end. Not yet at least. I really wanted to see his brown eyes light up again. I really wanted to hear his laugh again. And I really wanted to smell his cinnamon scent again. "Sure. I've never been there, but I've always wanted to go."

"Great! How about next week, the day after Christmas? I'll send you the details. There's something special I want to show you."

"Ok, sounds fun!" A rush of anticipation filled my body.

As we left the coffee shop and paused under a glowing streetlamp, I found myself in an awkward dilemma. *What do people do at the end of dates? Another handshake would be too formal. But a hug would be too...forward.*

I quickly formulated my exit plan. To avoid anything physical, I swung my purse in front of my body like a shield and occupied my hands by fishing out my keys. Then, before Arthur even knew what was happening, I power-walked to my car. Without breaking my stride, I turned around to yell, "Goodbye!"

I could only guess what Arthur was thinking as I left him in the dust. "Homeschooler, for sure."

THREE
BUTTERFLIES

The road to Woodland Park was lined with trees, and I found myself humming as I took in the scenery—it was such a pleasant change from being cooped up at home or in my classroom. I arrived in the parking lot a few minutes early, and I spotted Arthur in his car waiting for me. He had arrived even earlier than me, just like he had on our first date. I smiled to myself. *I guess we're both obsessed with being on time.*

My red wool jacket was perfect for the sunny, but brisk December afternoon weather. As I stepped out of my car, gravel crunched beneath my brown leather boots. Boots that I had bought with my refund money after I'd canceled my online dating subscription. *Maybe I'll get boots and a guy out of this deal!*

"Hi Sarah! It's so good to see you again." Arthur emerged from his Camry and greeted me with a friendly wave.

I looked him over from head to toe.

There had been a fuzzy haze around our first date in the coffee shop, but now I was confronted with the real-life version of Arthur. He looked so...regular. There was nothing trendy about his worn jeans or his black fleece jacket. He definitely wasn't some hip, 20-something-year-old with a six-pack. But, I reminded myself, that wasn't what I was looking for anyway.

My thoughts were interrupted when I noticed that Arthur was motioning to me. "There's something I'd like to show you. Follow me." He led me down a dirt trail into a grove of tall eucalyptus trees. The green leaves created a natural ceiling above us and I breathed in the sweet and woody fragrance.

"Look up," he whispered.

I lifted my eyes and gasped. Hundreds and hundreds of monarch butterflies clustered together among the branches. Some fluttered through the air like fairies, flashing their brilliant orange and black wings against the blue sky. I stood completely still and silent, enchanted by the magical sight. I didn't even want to blink for fear of missing one second.

"I've never seen anything like this before," I whispered breathlessly as I slowly turned in a full circle to see every angle.

"They're only here for a short time during their winter migration. I'm so glad you were able to come today."

"Me, too."

"When you're ready, there's another place I want to show you."

Curious, I followed Arthur down another winding

path until we reached a lush, grassy field. In the middle stood a white gazebo with a shingled roof and intricate lattice designs. Manicured bushes encircled it, and a stone fountain gently bubbled nearby. It looked like something out of a fairytale.

Once we drew closer, Arthur suggested that we sit and take a break on the benches underneath the gazebo. Without hesitation, he slid close to me, close enough that I caught another whiff of his cinnamon scent. My heart thudded a little faster. For an average-looking guy, Arthur certainly knew how to turn on the romance.

He turned to face me, giving me his full attention with his soft brown eyes. "I'd love to hear more about your parents and siblings."

"Well, my mom is Caucasian and my dad is Mexican-American, and they've been married for over 30 years. I have four amazing siblings. Growing up, we spent a lot of time together, so even today, we're very close-knit. What about you?"

"My parents are ethnically Chinese, and they immigrated to the United States before I was born. I'm an only child and they made a lot of sacrifices to give me a better life. Unfortunately, they split up when I was in college."

"Do your parents live nearby?" I asked.

"My dad lives a few cities away, and my mom and I own a house together, not too far from here."

"Oh." A red flag started to wave. It was one thing for me, a young woman in her 20s, to still live at home, but a man in his 30s? That probably wasn't helping his dating prospects.

"So, you're an English teacher, right?" Arthur continued to gaze at me as if I were the most interesting person he'd ever met. "I would love to hear more about your work."

"I work at a private Christian school, and I teach English to international students from China. I don't speak Mandarin or anything, but it's been fun to learn about my students' culture." I often thought about how ironic it was that I, a homeschooler, had chosen to become a teacher. Nevertheless, it was an arena where my love of rules, structure, and planning was able to shine. Besides, witnessing the transformation of my students year in and year out, brought a sense of hopefulness that anyone was capable of growth with the right encouragement.

"I bet your students love having you for a teacher."

"Aw, thanks." My cheeks flushed. "What do you do for work?"

"That's a good question." He stood up and began to pace around the gazebo. "I'm a marketing analyst, but I'm actually not working right now. I quit my last job a year ago, and I'm taking some time off. I like to think of it as a personal sabbatical."

"I see." *He's also unemployed? Yikes! No wonder he's still single.*

"It's been good to take a break and have more time to invest in dating."

"Well, that's definitely unconventional. But at least you're not a workaholic like me. I put in way too many hours at my job!"

"Hey, I'd be happy to help you find some work-life

balance. There are so many fun things to do around here. Speaking of, do you want to see the farm animals before we leave?"

"Um...ok." Animals were not exactly my cup of tea, but I could try and be a good sport for Arthur's sake.

As we wandered past a noisy chicken coop and a pen full of wooly sheep, I tried to restrain myself from wrinkling my nose. A new concern entered my mind. *Oh man, I bet he's an animal lover! That could be an issue if he's dating me. I have to find out more!*

"Do you have any pets?" I asked as nonchalantly as possible.

"No, I don't. Do you?"

"Well, we had a cat, but she passed away recently." It didn't seem appropriate to mention that the cat and I had been near enemies. I definitely didn't miss those sharp claws! Claws that she often swiped in my direction.

"Oh! I'm so sorry!" Arthur exclaimed with a furrowed brow. "Were you close?"

Were we close? That's definitely a question an animal lover would ask. I tried to answer diplomatically, "It was just a family cat, so you know, not that close."

"I see."

For the first time all day, an awkward silence settled over us and neither of us seemed to know what to say next. A cold breeze was picking up, so we turned toward the path back toward the parking lot. As we walked, I started a pros and cons list in my mind. *Pros: he's punctual, he's a good conversationalist, and he has a sweet, romantic side.*

Cons: he's unemployed, he lives with his mom, and he probably wants a whole house full of pets.

Why couldn't dating be more straightforward, like grammar rules? I wanted Arthur to be a clear right or wrong choice. I wasn't expecting so much nuance. Instead of butterflies dancing in my stomach, a serpent wriggled around in my gut. Fear whispered in my ear, "There's too much uncertainty with this guy. Go back to your life of comfort and predictability."

By the time I reached my car, my feet and forehead were throbbing. Giving a curt goodbye, I was just about to unlock my door when Arthur spread out his arms for a hug. I hesitated. *A hug? I don't even know how I feel about you yet.* I didn't want to mislead him by showing more interest than I actually felt. There was only one thing to do —I leaned in for a good, old-fashioned side-hug. The soft fleece of his jacket brushed against my cheek and the warmth of his chest was surprisingly...inviting. But I quickly shook away these thoughts.

A flicker of concern passed over Arthur's face, perhaps due to my sudden aloofness, and he softly asked, "I'll see you again soon, right?"

God, help me to be brave. While I still had doubts, I wanted to learn more about this unemployed, but very endearing man. I just needed some objective advice. Who would be brutally honest?

A sudden burst of inspiration struck me. "Hey, would you like to have dinner with my family next week?"

"Absolutely!"

"Prepare to be grilled." I flashed him a playful smile.

FOUR
THE IT GUY

I never thought the day would come when I would be bringing home a boy for dinner! I smiled as I wiped off our large dining room table and squeezed in an extra chair and place setting. So much had changed over the past few years to bring me to this point. My mind flashed back to when I was 14 years old. While sitting at this very table, I had heard some news that would change the rest of my life.

It had been a Saturday morning like any other. My four siblings and I had gathered around the table for breakfast with the usual flurry of cereal boxes, milk, and toast while spring sunshine filtered through the windows.

As I dug into my bowl of cereal, my dad cleared his throat above the hubbub. "I have some important news to tell you." He exchanged a silent glance with my mom. "We are removing our family from the Institute. Immediately. Starting today."

The only audible sound was that of chewing as we processed this information.

"Why?" My oldest brother, Bryan, was the first to find his voice.

"We read a book that exposed many serious problems with the group." My dad frowned. "Turns out, the leader is not who he seems to be. He's dictating a high standard of conduct, but he's not even living it out behind closed doors. This is not true Christianity. We actually think it's a cult."

A cult? Denial hit me first. I thought all cult members wore hooded robes, lived in a compound, and performed strange rituals. We certainly weren't like that! And yet, we were a bit peculiar. We definitely raised some eyebrows with our matching navy-blue-and-white outfits, our long lists of rules, and our unquestioning obedience to our leader.

"Are we still going to be homeschooled?" my younger brother, Sam, questioned between bites of toast.

"Yes, but with a different group," my dad answered.

"Do we still have to follow all those strict rules?" My younger sister, Grace, rolled her eyes.

"We want to honor God and follow the Bible, but we can toss some of those extra rules out the window!" My dad laughed aloud, a laugh that was giddy and child-like.

But I didn't laugh with him.

The firm foundation of my life swayed beneath my feet. For my entire childhood, I had molded my identity around this group. I was a rule-follower and a good person. This is how I stayed in God's favor. Now I wasn't sure who

I was, or what I was supposed to do to avoid plunging into disaster.

As the ramifications dawned on us, my siblings' questions picked up in intensity, just like a bag of popcorn kernels popping in the microwave.

"Can we wear jeans to church?" Rebekah, the baby of the family, hesitantly asked.

"Yes."

"Can we listen to Christian rock music?" Sam asked with a little more confidence.

"Yes."

"Can we eat pork?" Bryan licked his lips.

"Yes."

"Can we go trick-or-treating?" Rebekah's hopeful eyes sparkled.

"Yes."

"Can we get Internet access that's not censored?" Bryan folded his hands together and begged.

"Yes."

"Can we date?" Grace, the boldest of us all, audaciously asked.

"Yes, when you're old enough."

My mouth dropped to the floor upon hearing this answer. *But what about courtship and chaperoned dates? That sounds like a safer option, right?* I felt like an infant with her swaddle stripped away. I didn't know how to handle this new, destabilizing freedom. There was only one thing to do—postpone dating for as long as possible.

And I had. Until now.

Ding dong! The doorbell snapped me back to the present.

Before I had a chance to react, my mom raced from the kitchen to the front door. My dad followed a few steps behind, still wearing an oil-splashed apron.

"Remember, I need your honest opinion!" I called out after them.

My mom swung open the door. "It's so nice to meet you! Please come in!" She welcomed Arthur with a big hug.

I laughed to myself. *Did my mom just give Arthur a frontal hug before I did? I guess I have some catching up to do.*

"Here, I brought this for your family!" Arthur offered my mom a bag of fancy, foiled-covered chocolates.

"Thank you!" She gleefully accepted the package. "I love chocolate."

There goes her objectivity. I rolled my eyes. *At least I can still count on my dad to keep a clear head.*

My dad stepped forward to give Arthur a friendly, but reserved, handshake and then he introduced him to my brothers and sisters who stared in disbelief. Then we all took our seats around the table, with Arthur beside me. After my dad prayed, we began to eagerly pass around stacks of warm, flour tortillas. From the large selection of fillings—seasoned meat, rice, beans, cheese, and salsa—we stuffed and folded our bulging burritos and then hungrily devoured them.

"I've never had homemade Mexican food before," Arthur exclaimed as he filled his burrito and rolled it up.

However, once he lifted it to take a bite, all the contents spilled out the bottom onto his plate, causing my siblings to giggle. He was about to pick up a fork when my dad stopped him.

All eyes shifted to watch what would happen next.

"Arthur, can I give you a burrito rolling lesson?" my dad offered.

"Sure, I could use one," Arthur agreed.

Step-by-step, my dad demonstrated how to fold in the ends of the tortilla before rolling it up, and Arthur caught on immediately, creating a near-perfect burrito. My dad rewarded him with a beaming smile.

As we ate, our usual dinner conversation ramped up, filled with banter, kicks under the table, and uproarious laughter. Arthur seemed to have no problem jumping right in. He laughed at all of our jokes, even my brother's absurd ones, and made a point to talk to everyone at the table. Growing up with such a loud, multiple-conversations-happening-at-once kind of family, I never imagined there would be a man, let alone an only child like Arthur, who could keep up with all of the verbal chaos. Even the rapid fire of questioning by all seven of us wasn't enough to faze him.

"So, what are your hobbies, Arthur?" my dad asked.

"I like computers and technology. I'm actually a huge geek."

"Oh really?" Rebekah lit up. "Dad, ask him about our problem!"

"What's up?" Arthur leaned forward and rubbed his hands together, ready for a challenge.

"Our Wi-Fi doesn't work very well," my dad explained. "It's slow and it only works in the center of the house—it doesn't even reach the bedrooms."

"Yeah," my brothers chimed in. "Our bedrooms are total dead zones!"

"Ok, let me run a speed test to check your Internet speed." Arthur whipped out his phone and pulled up an app. After running his test, he declared, "Yes, I can clearly see that your Wi-Fi is slow. Would you mind showing me where your router is? We can do a little troubleshooting."

Dinner forgotten, my dad and Arthur left the table and headed toward the home office, like two cowboys riding off into the sunset together. I decided to follow at a distance, so as to not interrupt the process.

I could overhear Arthur talking, but I could barely understand all the technical jargon. "When your router is in this office, it's blocked by this wooden door. We can optimize the Wi-Fi coverage by moving it into the living room. Then the signal can reach the bedrooms."

"Great idea," my dad replied.

"And since you have so many people and devices in this house, I suggest upgrading to a more powerful router. I can email you a recommendation. Stepping into the living room, Arthur studied the TV, and popped his head behind the screen. "Do you stream shows using Wi-Fi, too?"

"Yeah."

"That's probably slowing things down. I can wire your TV with an Ethernet cable so it's not sucking up your Wi-Fi."

"An Ethernet cable?" My dad scratched his head.

"Don't worry, I have an extra one I can give you. With just a few tweaks, I think we can solve your problem."

My dad gazed at Arthur as if he were some kind of tech magician. "Can you please come back next Saturday and help me set everything up?"

I giggled in disbelief. *Who's asking who on a date now?*

"Sure! I'd love to come again." Arthur walked over to where I was observing them. "If that's ok with you, Sarah?"

"Of course!" This man had somehow managed to sweep my whole family off of their feet. He brought a sense of newness and fresh energy, and I wanted to see more. Had I given into my fear, I wouldn't have experienced this special evening. He was a blessing to my whole family. Sure, I still had lingering doubts, but I was certain that I still had lots of time before I had to really figure out my feelings.

Later that evening, as I walked Arthur to the door, I finally leaned in for a hug. A real hug with my arms and heart wide open. But as our bodies parted, a shadow seemed to pass over Arthur's face betraying an underlying anxiousness.

"Before I come visit here again, let me take you out for dinner, just the two of us. There's something I need to tell you."

FIVE
SURPRISE

Everything was perfect. The table next to the window. The steaming plates of pasta with grated parmesan cheese on top. The Italian music piping through the speakers. And the breadsticks! How had I lived my whole life without trying restaurant breadsticks?

After leaving the Institute, I had still chosen to live a small, but safe life. I was like a bird that remained in a cage even though the door was cracked open. Teaching consumed all of my time, and I hadn't taken the time to explore many attractions or restaurants. As a result, every new date with Arthur was a thrilling feast for my senses.

I glanced over at Arthur who, for some reason, didn't seem to be enjoying the date as much as I was. He shifted in his seat and looked about as comfortable as a cat on a hot tin roof.

I tried making small talk. "You'll be happy to hear that I'm starting to set some limits on my work, and I actually left school at a decent hour today. You're becoming a good influence on me."

"That's good to hear."

Silence.

I tried another topic. "These breadsticks are amazing! You know, second to Mexican food, bread is my favorite food." I took a big bite to prove my point.

"Wow, really?" Arthur seemed to consider this. "I know this local bakery that makes great sandwiches. Maybe we can go there sometime."

"That would be great."

Silence again.

With nothing else to say, I looked down at my plate and busied myself by twirling pasta around my fork.

"There's something I need to tell you," Arthur finally blurted out.

My eyes snapped up to his face.

"So, I'm actually interested in two women. There's you, and there's another woman who I've been seeing that lives a few cities away."

What? I felt like the wind had been knocked out of me and I immediately lost my appetite. *There's not just me?*

"I felt like I needed to tell you, in the interest of full disclosure." He spoke carefully, measuring every word. "I know you're new to dating, so maybe you don't know that people sometimes date multiple people at the same time while they're in the early stages. But once they agree to become exclusive, they just focus on one person."

"Oh. I didn't know that." Frustration at my own naivety, annoyance at Arthur, and jealousy towards this other woman boiled together into a bitter stew. I quickly turned my face toward the window as I regained my composure.

"Let me back up." Arthur pushed aside his plate as if to clear the table and to clear the air. "A few months ago, my ex-girlfriend and I broke up, so I started online dating again. Like I told you, I go on lots of first dates to keep my odds up because usually things don't work out after one or two dates. To be honest, I'm usually the one getting dumped."

Ah, yes. I recalled our first date when he had told me about "the numbers game."

"Anyway, I met this woman online and she kept wanting to see me. But I wasn't totally sure about her yet, so I kept my dating account open. Then a few weeks later...I met you."

My brows shot up in surprise. *I'm the other woman?* I suddenly realized that my anger and jealousy were not completely justified. This lady had every right to be mad at *me*. And mad at Arthur for adding me on. Although, in reality, Arthur wasn't bound to either of us.

Clearly uneasy, Arthur rubbed the back of his neck. "I've never been in this situation with two women, uh, lasting this long, at the same time. So, I'm trying to be up front and tell you both. And eventually, I'll have to make a decision to exclusively date one of you."

My hands clutched my water glass, trying to cool and steady myself. "So, what's she like?"

"She's around my age, in her 30s. She's marriage minded like I am."

"I see." With a twinge of envy, I pictured a sophisticated woman sipping coffee in a cafe and flipping through wedding magazines.

"But this is a hard dilemma because I really like *you*." Arthur looked deeply into my eyes. "I've enjoyed spending time with you and all of our great conversations. Plus, your family is amazing! They're so warm and welcoming. But I'm not really sure where you stand with wanting to get married..." His voice trailed off expectantly, giving me a chance to respond.

It suddenly hit me like a bolt of lightning: Arthur was trying to figure out which woman was more likely to make it down to the altar! Here I was, an inexperienced, 25-year-old side-hugger who had been in a cult. No wonder he wasn't sure about me. I wasn't even sure about me!

Arthur finally took a more direct approach. *"Do* you want to get married?"

His bluntness took me aback, but I wasn't going to be intimidated. I was in an unexpected job interview and even if I wasn't sure that I wanted the position, I wasn't going to blow it. Chin raised, I met his gaze. "Yes, I do want to get married...someday."

"Do you want kids?"

"Sure. Possibly two or three kids. You?"

"I'd like one or two. I've always wanted to be a father."

Now it was my turn to ask some blunt questions. I pressed the tips of my fingers together and narrowed my eyes at Arthur. "Why aren't you married yet? Why aren't things working out for you?"

"Man, I wish I knew!" Arthur gave a light chuckle and

leaned back in his seat. "Every woman has different values. Some women want a tall man or a highly educated man. Some women just want to date for fun, but don't want to get married. And some women take off running when they find out I'm just an unemployed bum."

A small smile escaped my lips until I reined it back in line.

"But seriously, all of my experiences, good and bad, have helped me clarify what I value in a relationship."

"And what's that?"

"The most essential thing I'm looking for is someone who is strong in their faith. Second, I believe that time is a precious resource. I always try to be on time and I'm looking for someone who values that, too. Money is also important, and I've dated women who spend almost everything they make. So I'm also looking for someone who is fiscally responsible."

Did he just use the word "fiscally" in a sentence? His vocabulary impressed the English geek in me. But that was beside the point. Even though Arthur appeared very different from me, I was surprised to learn that we both shared the same core values. It was almost as if I had met a long-lost extension of myself.

"There's one other little thing," Arthur said hesitantly. "It's not as important as the other ones. It's just a preference, and not a very popular one."

"This has got to be good." I leaned forward. "The more caveats the better! What is it?"

Arthur took a quick glance around the restaurant and then lowered his voice to a whisper. "To be honest, I don't like cats or dogs. I'm allergic to them. I've dated some people who were *really* into their pets. And let's just say, it didn't quite work out."

"But I thought you loved animals!" I accused him. "You took me to Woodland with all those farm animals! And you seemed so emotional when I told you that my cat passed away!"

"I was just trying to be sympathetic," Arthur defended himself. "I was concerned that *you* loved pets."

"No way! I never want pets!"

Our eyes locked for an instant, then we both dissolved into laughter. Deep, hysterical, clutch-your-stomach-laughter. We kept trying to stop laughing, to no avail, which made us both laugh even harder.

As much as I wanted to savor the moment, I finally willed my unruly body back under control and scolded myself for letting down my guard so easily. I had to get a hold of myself before this guy got under my skin! I cleared my throat, and murmured, "Well, I'm glad we got that cleared up. Hey, it's getting late and I better head home soon."

"Already?" The joyful abandon disappeared from Arthur's face. He flagged down the server and paid for our meal. "Well, thanks for having dinner with me tonight and for listening. I know this puts you in an awkward position." He gave me a sheepish smile which I refused to admit looked kind of cute.

"It's better to know than not to know." Gathering my things, and all the pieces of my heart, I quickly rose from my seat and said a polite goodbye.

SIX

CALLING DIBS

"The nerve of this guy!" I pounded my fist on Zia's kitchen table where we sat drinking tea the day after Arthur's bombshell revelation. "Can you believe he's dating two women at once?"

"Actually, it's quite common." Zia, dressed stylishly in a matching velour pants set, didn't seem fazed at all by the news. She paused to calmly stir honey into her chamomile tea. "Steven was dating several ladies before he finally came to his senses and went exclusive with me."

"But what if I invest more into Arthur, and then he just waltzes away with the other girl?" I crossed my arms over my sweatshirt. Already, I could sense Fear wrapping its scaly body around my heart like an impenetrable shield. Sure, he might squeeze the life out of me, but at least I'd be safe.

"News flash! Love is risky." Zia let out a small laugh. "There's always a chance of being rejected. But it's worth the risk."

I held up my hand like a stop sign. "Well, I'm just going to slow things down and start giving him the cold shoulder until I know if he's committed."

"Sarah," Zia sighed and shook her head. "You're going 30 miles per hour in a 65 zone. You can't go any slower! Besides, if you start to withdraw, he'll think you're not interested."

"I just don't know how I really feel about him yet! This is more complicated than I thought!" I brought my knees up to my chest and lowered my head onto them.

Zia patted my arm. "It's ok. You don't have to have it all figured out yet. But from what you've already told me, it sounds like he's got some solid qualities. And there's definitely some connection between you two."

I hated to admit that she was right. Indeed, there was something magical about our lively conversations and effortless connection. I smiled as I thought about the way Arthur looked at me, really looked at me, when I spoke, as if he were seeing straight into my soul.

"Let me read you a verse." Zia picked up her worn Bible from the table and flipped a few pages to Romans 12:9 which she read aloud. "Love must be sincere. Hate what is evil; cling to what is good."

"Hmm, explain more." I took another sip of tea as I mulled over the verse.

"I think it means that love should be genuine. If you love someone, you should show it by your actions. And we should cling tightly to things that are good."

Like Arthur. Sure, it was a risk to put my heart out there, but there was just too much goodness to walk away now. I didn't want to lose him. This wasn't the time to retreat—this was the time to step on the accelerator and declare my interest. But how?

I considered my options. A text? A card? No, I needed to do something bolder to get his attention. What would a heroine in a romance story do?

A kiss. I have to kiss him.

FOR THE REST of the week, the only thought that dominated my mind was that I needed to kiss Arthur. Not on the lips or anything. Goodness, I wasn't *that* brazen. Just a peck on the cheek would do the trick to throw my hat in the ring. One slight problem—I had never kissed a guy in my life, but I was confident that I could figure it out with some quick research on the Internet. Which is, of course, what one does to learn about all things related to physical affection.

Finally, Saturday afternoon arrived.

Back and forth, I paced the living room while Arthur and my dad fiddled around with a jumble of cables that resembled the jumble of nerves inside of me. *What's taking them so long?* After an hour or so, they high fived each other and showed off the improved Wi-Fi range, much to my siblings' delight. During dinner, I bulked up on extra servings of my mom's lasagna, knowing that I would need sustenance for the task ahead. My siblings brought out a stack of board games, but I mostly just twirled a strand of hair around my finger, not even trying to win. There was a bigger game at stake tonight.

After the last round of Apples to Apples, Arthur excused himself to leave. "Thanks for a fun time. Wish I could stay longer, but I'm heading to the evening service at my church."

This was my cue to spring into action.

"I'll walk you to your car!" I quickly stood and escorted Arthur out the door. As we stepped out onto the front porch, I firmly closed the front door behind me. *I just need a little privacy away from my family.*

The sun had started to set, reds and oranges streaking the sky. Tonight was definitely the night. I reviewed the steps that I had mentally rehearsed 100 times. *All I have to do is lean in for a hug, then I can land my kiss once his face is close to mine. Simple and straightforward.*

I took a deep breath. It was now or never. I extended my arms, but somehow only one arm got around his body. Arthur seemed to think I was going for a side-hug, so he responded with a side-hug. There I stood, tucked under his arm, and I had no access to his cheek. Arg! After our awkward embrace, he climbed into his car and disappeared around the corner. *He probably thinks I don't like him at all. I'm going to lose him forever!*

I shuffled inside and sprawled out on the couch in defeat. Immediately, Fear snaked its heavy body onto my chest and began to berate me, "You're the lamest dater in the world. Arthur is definitely better off with the other woman. Just let him go." But before I could fully spiral into self-condemnation, my thoughts were interrupted by my mom rushing past me.

"Oh, hi Sarah. I'm going to take off now, but I'll see you later." She grabbed her keys and started heading out the door. "I'm visiting my cousin in the hospital."

I suddenly remembered that Arthur's church was near the hospital. "Wait!" A plan quickly formulated in my mind and I bolted upright, letting Fear tumble to the floor. "I'm coming with you!"

As my mom and I drove on the freeway, I knew it was time to bare my soul. I wasn't accustomed to talking to her about boys and the inner workings of my heart, but desperate times called for desperate measures. I told her all about Arthur, the other woman he was dating, and my lame side-hugs. "I need to tell him how I feel before it's too late."

"Alright! Let's do it!" My mom grinned ear to ear and stepped on the gas. Unlike me, she actually seemed to be enjoying this escapade.

I tried calling Arthur, but his phone was off. *Probably because he's in church.* The next best option was to text him. "We need to talk. Can I meet you after your service ends?"

After sending my message, I waited for what seemed like an eternity. Goosebumps covered my arms. Breathing became more difficult. The lasagna churned in my stomach. At age 25, I was finally catching up on all the teenage angst and drama that I had missed out on.

Ding! My screen lit up with Arthur's reply: "Sure." He also sent the address.

One hour later, after a quick visit at the hospital, we pulled into the parking lot of Arthur's church. My legs wobbled underneath me as I exited the car. Rolling down the window, my mom called out after me, "Take all the time you need! I'm totally fine here!" With that, she pulled out a book and settled in for a cozy reading session.

The sky was now pitch black and the air was chilly. Nevertheless, I was sweating as if I had just run a marathon. I pulled my hair into a messy bun and fanned myself with my hand. I glanced to my right and left, disoriented by the unfamiliar location. *Where could Arthur be?* Bright lights glowed around the church entrance and I headed in that direction. I finally spotted my target and sprinted toward him. "Arthur, we need to talk," I said breathlessly.

"Is everything ok?" Arthur's forehead wrinkled into worry lines. "What's going on?"

I jumped right into my speech before I lost my nerve. "I know you're seeing another woman and I'm sure she's amazing. And I know that I can come off a little reserved. But I want to make it clear that I...I actually *do* like you." I gave a shy smile. "And I really hope that you can be part of my life."

Arthur let out a long breath, and his worry lines disappeared. "Thank you for sharing your feelings with me, Sarah. When I saw your text, I thought that you were going to dump me. It's happened so many times before. Women will usually tell me that they're only interested in me as a brother-in-Christ." He shook his head as if remembering past rejections. Then he looked directly at me, as if seeing me with new eyes, eyes that shone with undeniable affection. "Will you let me walk you back to your car?"

"Yes, I'd like that."

As we strolled through the moonlit parking lot, Arthur gently wrapped his arm across my shoulders. At first, I stiffened in shock. But after a moment, my muscles relaxed under the warmth of his body and his signature cinnamon scent enlivened my senses. It was both strange and wonderful to be in such close proximity to Arthur. It was like witnessing lightning in the sky—a little terrifying but also breathtaking.

Once we reached my mom's car, I said good night and I opened my arms for a hug. This time I got both arms around him, and I knew that it was time to seal the deal. While still embracing, I slightly turned my face towards him and placed a soft kiss on his cheek. *Smooch!*

Then I jumped into my mom's getaway car as fast as I could. As we sped off, I snuck a quick peek to see Arthur looking surprised, but with a smile a million miles wide. Now the ball was in his court. I would just have to wait and see which woman Arthur would choose.

SEVEN
LEVELING UP

The aroma of sourdough bread filled my senses as I entered the bakery-cafe where Arthur had asked me to meet him for dinner. I was still dressed in my work slacks and a sweater, but at least I had on a cute lacy blouse. Amazingly, I had managed to arrive earlier than Arthur, and I used the extra time to peek into the display cases. My tummy rumbled as I admired the golden loaves of bread with glistening crusts. Some loaves were even shaped like teddy bears! Involuntarily, I started salivating.

Then bells over the door jingled, signaling Arthur's arrival. "Hi Sarah!" He caught me ogling the displays and chuckled.

I turned to face him. "What is this magical place? It's like bread heaven!"

"You mentioned that you loved bread, so I had a feeling you would like it. Order whatever you want!"

I blushed with delight that he had remembered that small detail about me.

At the counter, I ordered a roast beef sandwich on toasted sourdough, and Arthur insisted on buying a few extra loaves for me to take home for my family. We found a quiet corner, and Arthur pulled out my chair for me, always the perfect gentleman. And so began yet another date in the fragile and uncertain zone of not-yet-exclusive.

We had been in this zone for the past few weeks. Although it was fun to go out, the issue of Arthur dating two women had hovered over us like a brewing storm cloud. Inevitably, one of us was going to get dumped, but I wasn't sure which way it was going to go. Nevertheless, I was determined to hold my ground and stick it out until the bitter end.

Hunger pangs forced me to push aside my worries and dig into my sandwich with a satisfying *crunch*. I closed my eyes to focus more on the taste. The bread was tangy and delicious and paired perfectly with the tender, salty roast beef. When I finally opened my eyes again, I realized that Arthur was gazing at me.

"I love that you appreciate the simple things," he commented.

"I do! I feel like I'm just now starting to really live my life. Besides, this sandwich is the best," I exclaimed in between bites. "You should try yours."

"Well, there's actually something I wanted to talk to you about."

Oh snap. I swallowed a big chunk of bread but managed to not choke. It was time to find out my fate.

"Would you like to start dating exclusively?" Arthur

looked directly into my eyes and gave a sweet, hopeful smile.

My heart rate sped up a few notches. This was indeed the outcome that I had been hoping for, but now that it was here, I wasn't sure if I was ready. Funny how that works. I let out a long breath. Even though I was scared, deep down, I knew that I wanted to take the next step. The commitment of exclusivity would give me confidence to move a little closer and open up more. And God would be with me, as He always had been.

"Yes," I finally replied. "I would love to!"

"Alright!" Arthur's smile widened and he reached across the table to gently take my hand in his. With his thumb, he drew small circles on my palm. His warm, soft touch caused my breathing to slow and a sense of peace spread throughout my body.

"Sarah," he said softly, "I know we are good together. You are different from anyone I've ever dated."

"But what about the other woman?" I bit my lip with concern as I suddenly considered her. *Will she ever meet her prince charming?*

"I'll meet with her tomorrow and let her know my decision. It's never easy to have these conversations, but I believe she'll find an even better match eventually. Besides, I've been leaning towards you ever since I first met you. I just wasn't sure if you were interested in me. That is, until you, uh, kissed me."

My cheeks reddened, but inwardly I was proud.

"Speaking of that topic, now that we are official, I have two things to ask you," Arthur finally released my hand, but his gaze didn't leave my face. "First, what boundaries are you comfortable with in terms of physical affection?"

I shifted in my chair. Growing up, there was so much emphasis on *not* thinking about guys, *not* doing anything physical with them, and *not* falling into temptation. As a result, I had never considered what affection was ok or even what I liked.

Sensing my hesitation, Arthur offered, "How about I start?"

"Yes, go ahead. I need more time to think." I took a sip of water.

Arthur jumped right in, having clearly thought this out beforehand. "Well, I want to save sex for marriage. But I'm ok with kissing and making out."

I wiped my sweaty hands on my pants. Sure, I was also on board with saving sex for marriage, but there was a whole realm of fuzzy, gray areas outside of that. There weren't enough rules, and a lack of rules was a sure-fire trigger for me. Still, I tried to keep my voice light, "Let's just stick with hugs and some kisses on the cheek. And then we can revisit the topic of kissing on the lips in a few months?"

Arthur gave me an understanding look. "Whatever you're comfortable with is fine with me."

"Thanks." I breathed a sigh of relief that Arthur was willing to go at my pace, even if it was only a bit faster than a snail's. Eager to change the subject, I inquired, "By the way, what was the second thing you wanted to ask me?"

"Oh yeah, I almost forgot. I wanted to invite you to visit my house and meet my mom on Saturday."

"I would love to meet her!" If she was anything like her son, I was sure that she would be delightful.

"But there's something you should know." Arthur's shoulders slumped. "My mom might not like you."

"Why? She doesn't even know me."

"I think she prefers that I date Chinese women."

EIGHT
BEST FOOT FORWARD

I rocked back and forth in my high heels as I watched the florist prepare the bouquet of roses that I had painstakingly selected. With sharp scissors and decisive snips, she trimmed the tips of the stems at an angle. Next, she wrapped the flowers with tissue paper and added an outer layer of shiny cellophane. Finally, her nimble fingers tied a piece of ribbon into a beautiful bow.

"They're for my boyfriend's mother," I confided. "I'm meeting her today for the first time."

"Good luck." The florist winked.

"Thanks, I need it." I knew enough about Chinese culture from my students to know that it's always a good idea to bring a gift when visiting someone's home. Probably even more so if there's a chance they might not like you.

I drove to the address that Arthur had given me and found a tidy-looking, single- story house. I parked in front but didn't get out of my car. Arthur's warning played over and over in my head, just as it had all week. Part of me wanted to just drive away and avoid any potential conflict. Who was I to come between Arthur and his mom? I didn't want to end up in a forbidden romance like Romeo and Juliet—clearly that hadn't ended well.

However, God had already gotten me this far, and I figured that I just needed 60 more seconds of courage to get to the doorstep. "Dear God," I prayed. "You helped me get a boyfriend and we're just starting this new level of our relationship. Please don't let it all end here. Please help Arthur's mom to accept me for who I am."

With that, I smoothed my gray pencil skirt, opened the car door, and marched up the walkway to the porch. My finger rang the doorbell exactly at our scheduled meeting time.

Barely a second later, the door flew open and I found myself face-to-face with a petite woman who possessed the same sparkling brown eyes as Arthur. "Hello, I'm Laura."

"Hi, I'm Sarah. I brought these flowers for you." I remembered to offer them with two hands, as is proper tradition. Maybe if I followed all the rules, she would give me a chance.

"Thanks! I love roses." Laura's face lit up. "Please come in."

So far, so good. I gingerly stepped into the front entry-way, but before going any further, I slipped off my heels, exposing my bare feet.

"Oh, no need to remove your shoes." Laura waved her hands.

"I don't mind." I knew that above all, you *always*

remove your shoes before entering a Chinese home. And clearly I was right, since they had a brimming shoe rack next to the door.

"No, really, " Laura protested more forcefully. "Our hardwood floors are very cold." She was right—I could feel the chill seeping through the cracks.

"I'm more comfortable with my shoes off." I tried to sound convincing.

"You look cold." Laura shot an anxious look at my bare feet and legs that peeked out beneath my skirt.

No matter what she said, there was no way that I, the new non-Asian girlfriend, was about to break all cultural norms and wear shoes in their house. There could be serious repercussions. So I just froze in the entryway, like a scared animal, uncertain of my next move. *Yikes, I'm already getting off on the wrong foot.*

Fortunately, Arthur appeared from around the corner and motioned me to come in. "Hi Sarah! Please come in and sit down."

Leaving my shoes behind, I followed Arthur to the kitchen where I found a seat at the table. But as I glanced behind me, all I could see was Laura rushing away to another room. *Oh, no, I've really offended her now. Maybe I should have kept my shoes on. But that might have been offensive, too!*

I hung my head in despair. However, just a few minutes later, Laura reappeared. I glanced up to see her handing me a small, plastic covered package. Slippers. The kind a fancy spa might offer. I slipped them on, grateful for the added warmth. Next, Laura handed me a fluffy blanket which I draped over my lap. She had come up with the perfect solution to keep me cozy.

"Would you like some tea?" She pulled a few mugs out of the cabinets.

"Yes, please."

As she handed me the warm drink, her smile was even warmer, and I was taken aback by her friendliness. This wasn't at all what I was expecting. An aura of grace emanated from her. Grace which soothed my anxiety about having to prove myself. Grace which allowed me to take a deep breath. I hadn't considered the possibility she would be more concerned about my well-being than about her traditions. Perhaps Arthur was wrong about his mom.

Before long, the three of us were sitting around the table, sipping tea and chatting away like old friends.

"So, please tell me more about Arthur." I turned towards Laura. "I'd love to hear from a mother's perspective."

"I've been worried about Arthur for years." Laura patted her son on the shoulder. "He used to work long hours all the time, and he didn't have any friends or social life."

"Sadly, that's true," Arthur chimed in.

"But then he started going to church and became a Christian," Laura recounted. "He made some good friends and started getting out of the house more, but he still didn't have good luck with dating. He tried hard, but no one seemed right for him."

"It's not easy out there." Arthur shook his head.

"And then, to make matters worse, he quit his job!" Laura exclaimed. "I almost had a heart attack!"

"It wasn't a healthy work environment, and I needed some time to travel and explore and date," Arthur explained.

"But no one is going to date you if you're unemployed!" Laura shot back. "Right, Sarah?"

I laughed. "True, most women aren't into that. But I don't mind. Arthur's smart and he has great character. If I listed out all of his good qualities, it would be several pages long! I know he'll figure it out."

"I'm so grateful that you're giving him a chance." Laura looked directly at me. "To be honest, at first I wanted him to just date Chinese women. It would be nice to have someone who shares our family's background. But at this point, anyone who is willing to date my unemployed son must be pretty special. And from what Arthur has told me, you *are* special."

My body warmed with pleasure.

Arthur spoke up, "That's right. I'm always telling my mom that shared values are more important than shared culture. Especially when it comes to faith."

"I agree with that, too," I said.

"Well, I'm not a Christian." Laura pointed to herself. "But if Arthur ever gets married, I know it will be a miracle. Maybe I will even start to believe in God!"

We all laughed together, and I found myself falling in love with this sweet and spunky woman. Her acceptance was an answer to prayer, and I sensed an open door for more relationship building in the future.

"Ok." Laura rose to her feet. "I'll let you two have some alone time. It was nice to meet you, Sarah. Please come back again soon!"

"Thank you, I will!"

Once Laura was out of the room, Arthur scooted closer and swung his arm around me. He brushed my hair aside and softly murmured in my ear, "You know, Valentine's Day is coming up next Saturday. Will you be my date?"

My stomach fluttered. "I'll have to check my calendar," I joked. "Oh, wait. I just remembered I'm totally free."

I felt like a tourist about to celebrate a cultural holiday in a foreign country. Excited, yes. But I also couldn't help but wonder, *how does this actually work?*

NINE

VALENTINE'S DAY 101

Why did I buy this dress? I didn't realize it was so short! Mortified, I stared at my reflection in the full-length mirror in my bedroom. A few days before, I had spontaneously bought a pink, flouncy dress, but I should have tried it on sooner and not 15 minutes before Arthur was scheduled to pick me up. Any dress that hit above my knees made me feel like I was pushing the boundaries of modesty, and my old friend, Fear, wasted no time encircling my legs and shaming me with messages from my past. "Don't show too much skin! Don't draw attention to your body! You'll give Arthur the wrong idea!"

In a panic, I threw open my closet to peruse my safe, albeit drab, collection of professional work outfits. I slipped into a black dress with a high neckline and low hemline that probably would have been more appropriate to wear to a funeral. Checking my reflection again, I let out a groan. *Argh, this isn't right either. I'm no good at fashion.*

And I'm no good at dating! I'm already failing my first ever Valentine's Day date.

While debating if I should try on another outfit, the doorbell rang. My time was up. I double checked my purse to make sure I had my special gift for Arthur, then rushed to open the front door.

"Happy Valentine's Day!" Arthur greeted me with a peck on the cheek and a gigantic bouquet of flowers.

My first bouquet from a man. As I accepted the bundle, I breathed in the delicate fragrance and paused to tuck the moment into my heart. "Thank you. These are beautiful."

"You look beautiful, too." Arthur's earnest tone made me believe that he really meant it, despite my funeral dress. Affection can beautify anyone.

"Aww, thanks. You look great, too." Arthur looked quite dapper in his khaki pants and gray button up shirt, but it was his enthusiastic smile that added the cherry on top.

After placing my flowers in a vase of water, I followed Arthur to his car where he chivalrously opened the passenger door for me. Once seated, Arthur pulled up his calendar on his phone screen. "I have the whole afternoon planned out. I got us tickets to a musical, then afterwards we can browse some shops before our dinner reservations. How does that sound?"

"Fabulous!" As impressive as the date sounded, I was even more in awe of his organized digital calendar. How amazing to find a man who loved calendars and planning as much as I did!

Arthur tapped his phone again and launched a podcast app. "While we're driving, I thought we could listen to a podcast together." Voices buzzed over the car speakers as Arthur began driving down the road.

"What's this episode about?"

"It's about habits that can lead to a happy marriage," Arthur explained matter-of-factly. "I thought we could listen together and talk about it over dinner."

My stomach dropped. *Why was he bringing up the topic of marriage?* Sure, that's what I was ultimately searching for, too, but any thought of that seemed like a long, long way off. I was just trying to wrap my head around dating.

FOR THE NEXT FEW HOURS, I pushed aside my worries and got swept up in the music, dancing, and costumes of the musical. My cheeks were sore from smiling so much. After the final bows and thunderous applause, we threaded our way through the crowd out into the bustling downtown area.

Arthur checked his watch. "We still have time before our dinner reservation. Would you like to visit a good old-fashioned bookstore?"

"You know how to charm a teacher's heart!"

Arthur slipped his hand into mine and led me down the sidewalk past several quaint shops and restaurants. The streetlights flickered on, creating a soft glow and sparkle. We were surrounded by other couples who were also enjoying the romantic holiday with their fancy outfits and star-gazed expressions. They seemed to have it all figured out. And if anyone saw me, smiling hand-in-hand with my boyfriend, they would think that I had it all figured out, too. But anxiety sloshed beneath my calm exterior. *Does my black dress look too depressing? Am I holding Arthur's hand correctly? Am I supposed to flirt? Maybe I'll never figure this dating stuff out.*

Before long, we arrived at the bookstore and the crisp smell of new books drew me in. I was about to start browsing aimlessly when Arthur beckoned me to follow him. Curious, I quickened my pace as he wove around aisles until he finally stopped at a long shelf. I glanced at the sign hanging above: *Dating & Relationships.*

"Whenever I go to bookstores, I always check out this section. A few years ago, I didn't know the first thing about dating." He laughed at himself. "Believe it or not, I'm also an introvert, so I used to struggle with opening myself up and engaging people in conversation. Thankfully, I've been able to make some progress by reading books and listening to podcasts."

"But you make it look so easy!" I challenged him. "I thought you were just naturally good at dating. Unlike me."

"I had to learn and experiment and make mistakes, just like everyone else. That's how you get better at any skill. It just takes patience and persistence."

His words arrested me. This was a message that I often preached to my students, yet it sounded different coming from Arthur. If I were honest, I believed that I had a limited capacity for learning, especially when it came to dating and relationships, due to my sheltered background. But maybe there was hope, even for someone like me.

Arthur ran his finger across a row of colorful book spines. "I could recommend some books, if you're interested in learning more."

I paused to consider his idea. There was no pressure behind it, just a sincere desire to help me grow. I tilted my head sideways and scanned the titles which seemed to offer a plethora of practical, actionable advice. Although the thought of learning a new skill felt daunting, staying stuck in my own naivety and limited mindset didn't sound enjoyable either. This was my chance to gain some confidence. "Ok, I'm down. Give me your best picks."

CANDLELIGHT DANCED across our white tablecloth and violin music filled the air during our dinner at an upscale French restaurant. My salmon filet was perfectly tender and I savored every flaky bite. I finally pushed my plate away and wiped my mouth. "This is the nicest dinner I've ever had. Thank you."

"Thank *you* for being my date. I'm so happy you're here with me."

"Before I forget, I have a gift for you." I reached into my purse and pulled out a black leather book with a ribbon tied around it.

"Really?" Arthur's eyebrows jumped up, and he eagerly leaned forward. "I wasn't expecting anything."

"It's a special journal for you." I opened the first page. "I wrote a list of 100 things I admire about you. (1) You love God. (2) You plan great dates. (3) You are patient with me. (4) You helped my family fix their Wi-Fi. (5) You make me laugh." I handed him the book. "You can read the rest yourself."

As Arthur silently read, his face glowed like the morning sun and his smile seemed like it was going to burst. The more I got to know Arthur, the more I appreciated the little elements that made up his character. They were like the brushstrokes of a painting or the individual notes of a beautiful song. Other women may have just seen an average man sitting in front of them. But by looking closely, I was able to see the gold hidden within.

When Arthur finally reached the end of the list, he closed the book and held it to his chest. "No one has ever done anything like this for me. I'm really touched." He looked away and was quiet for a moment. I wasn't sure if his eyes were glistening with tears or if it was just the candlelight flickering across them. "Sarah." His eyes returned to my face. "Remember that podcast about marriage?"

"Yes." *How could I forget?*

"I'd like us to start exploring that topic more. After all, marriage is yet another skill that can be learned and developed."

"Um, ok."

"And by the way, speaking of that topic..." Arthur cleared his throat. "I just found out that my church is having a premarital class in a few weeks. I'd like to go, but it would be a shame to go alone. Would you come with me?" He looked at me with irresistible puppy eyes.

"A premarital class?" My mouth fell open and I briefly wondered if I was being pranked on a hidden camera show. But no, this was not a joke. In a split second, our tame kiddie ride had suddenly turned into a high-speed roller coaster, and I wasn't sure if I was brave enough to stay on.

Arthur tried to reassure me. "It doesn't mean we have to get married or anything. Just see it as a learning opportunity."

I met his gaze and slowly nodded yes. I couldn't quite explain what was happening, but my desire to grow, to burst forth from my cocoon, was growing stronger every day.

SPRING

TEN

THE CHAPERONES

I clicked open my work email and saw two words that no teacher wants to see: *chaperone duty*.

It was now several weeks after Valentine's Day, and yet, a resurgence of romance was in the air, as evidenced by the restless, hormonal highschoolers that roamed around campus making eyes at each other and whispering amongst their friends. This could mean only one thing—the Spring Prom was coming up.

And sure enough, I had been assigned to chaperone.

Instead of my usual curmudgeonly reaction to being assigned extra work, I found a smile creeping across my face as I sat at my desk and scanned the details. Growing up, I'd never had the chance to attend a prom, and I'd always been curious what happened at these magical and mysterious school dances. Perhaps I could live vicariously through my students.

Suddenly, a wild idea exploded in my mind—I could

invite Arthur to be my prom date! After all, he had invited me to a premarital class. Not that my idea was as crazy.

However, Fear promptly showed up to dismiss the idea. *"Nah, he wouldn't want to help chaperone a lame high school dance. And your principal wouldn't approve anyway."*

"Shut up!" I surprised myself with my boldness. This was my year to break out of my shell. And what better place to debut the new-and-improved version of myself than at prom.

With a surge of energy, I headed to the school office and tracked down the principal, Mrs. Strickland, whose blond hair remained perfectly coiffed into a bun, even after a full day of work.

Stammering and stuttering, I explained my idea, but she didn't look convinced.

"I'm not sure about this." She studied me with her steely blue eyes. "He'll probably be a distraction to you."

"I promise I'll be fully attentive. Besides, an extra chaperone would be helpful, right?"

"Fine," she sighed. "Let's give it a try."

"Thank you!" I tried my best to suppress the squeals that threatened to burst forth from my mouth.

IT IS A WELL-KNOWN fact that the best part of prom is the prom dress, and this time around, I was wise enough to ask Zia to lend me something from her extensive wardrobe. Wow, did she deliver!

As I prepared for the big night out, I retrieved the dress that had been patiently waiting in my closet all week. I took a deep breath and gently ran my hands over the bright red fabric. I lifted the dress over my head and slipped it over my body. The fitted, strapless top accentuated my curves, while the twirly skirt showed off my legs. I clasped on gold earrings and a chunky gold chain necklace, double checking that they were nickel-free to avoid an allergic reaction. Then I brushed out my long, dark hair and let it flow freely around my bare shoulders. As I turned slowly in front of the mirror, the sequins that covered the dress sparkled like diamonds. I had never seen this version of myself, and I couldn't help but marvel at the transformation. *Who is this woman?*

Even after leaving the Institute, I had continued to cover up my feminine form with loose-fitting blouses, thick sweaters, and jeans that were one size too big. Messages from my youth reinforced the idea that it was wrong to draw any attention to myself and that if I wasn't careful, I could cause men to stumble by my appearance. So just to be safe, I kept my body well-concealed and camouflaged.

But I was beginning to realize that my body was a gift, wonderfully created by God. Arbitrary rules about modesty were less important than the state of my heart. There was a time and place to appropriately display my beauty, and tonight was certainly one of them!

AS THE SUN was beginning to set, I arrived at the rented country club which was nestled in the hills overlooking the city. Near the entrance, I paused to get my bearings. Swarms of teenagers, dressed in suits and sparkly gowns, entered the stately building which was flanked by palm trees.

Soon enough, I saw Arthur emerge through the crowd wearing a black suit and shiny shoes, looking as giddy as a teenager himself. When he spotted me, he stopped in his tracks with an expression that I had never seen before. A look of wonder. "Wow," he said breathlessly. "You look beautiful!"

I gave a little twirl so he could see the entire dress. "Thanks for being my date."

Arthur wasted no time gathering me up in his arms for an embrace. Then he leaned in and pressed a warm, tingly kiss on my cheek.

"Hope that's ok." He gave me a playful grin. "We gotta give the students something to gossip about!"

"Just don't get too carried away or you'll get detention!" I teased back as I slipped my arm into his.

Once inside, we were greeted by Mrs. Strickland who handed out job assignment sheets to the chaperones. She reminded us of our duty to keep things under control and urged us to constantly rotate around the building with our eyes open for any signs of trouble.

As we started our rounds, Arthur narrowed his eyes and snapped into secret agent mode.

"Let's check out the refreshment table first. I better

taste all the drinks to make sure they're really non-alcoholic."

"I'm sure it's just soda!" I giggled and elbowed him in the ribs.

"Hey, look at the stairwell over there." Arthur pointed to a dark corner of the building. "I bet some students are making out. I'll go investigate!" He theatrically tip-toed closer to check it out, but no guilty suspects were found.

This continued for the next few hours, with Arthur relishing every opportunity to make me laugh. Despite my efforts to keep a straight face, I couldn't resist his humor. This was the most fun I'd ever had chaperoning a school event. A few students cast curious glances in our direction, surprised to see their teacher in a red dress. And with a man by her side.

Near the end of the night, Arthur proposed, "Let's go check the dance floor. We need to make sure there's no twerking or grinding going on."

"Shh!" I playfully poked him in the arm. "Don't give the students ideas."

We stood at the edge of the dance floor, and my eyes adjusted to the dimmed lighting. The latest pop song blared over the speakers, and I tapped my foot along to the beat. We got a kick out of watching the boys strutting their breakdance moves and the girls prancing around in their high heels. Heads bopped, hips twisted, and arms swayed with wild abandon.

The song finally ended, and a piano ballad began to play. Most of the teens sat down to take a break, but a few brave couples draped their arms around each other and started slow dancing. John Legend's voice came over the speakers crooning, "All of Me," and I felt the vibe in the room change from frenetic energy to sweet passion.

"Hey you two, get out there!" I felt a little shove and looked behind me. To my surprise, it was Mrs. Strickland with the slightest hint of a smile. "It's time for you to dance."

"Yes, ma'am!" I automatically responded.

We turned and faced each other, uncertain of what to do next. I glanced around at the other dancers and tried to copy their body positions. I guided Arthur's hands to encircle my waist, then I reached up to place my hands on his shoulders. They were solid and strong which gave me a sense of stability.

My dress swished against my bare legs as we swayed back and forth with the music. The disco ball lights patterned both our faces as we turned circles. Everyone else in the room melted away into the background and suddenly it was just me, a girl at prom dancing with her boyfriend, having the time of her life.

Without warning, I noticed Arthur's expression change. His jovial grin faded, and a fire seemed to blaze in his eyes. He squeezed my waist a little tighter. Ever so softly, he began singing the romantic lyrics, his voice low and husky. When he sang the line that all of him loved all of me, his meaning was unmistakable. He was singing the words directly to me.

Fear slithered down my spine and I slowed my sway. I turned my head and broke the too-intimate eye contact.

ELEVEN
CHEMISTRY EXPERIMENT

I think Arthur is falling in love with me. But am I in love with him? These anxious thoughts circled my mind as Arthur and I explored a local trail a few days after prom. It was a lovely April day with a pastel-blue sky sweeping above us. The mid-afternoon sun was warm and invigorating, and I was glad that I had dressed comfortably in jean shorts and a T-shirt.

Our steps naturally fell in sync on the dirt path, but I wasn't sure if our hearts were as aligned as our feet. Sure, I liked Arthur and enjoyed his friendship. Not many people could make me crack up laughing like he could! But I wasn't sure if my romantic feelings matched his.

As we came around a curve in the path, a large lake came into view. The crystal blue water shimmered in the sunshine as if a million diamonds were dancing on the surface.

"Let's get closer to get a better view." Arthur led me down a slope toward a wooden bench. Nearby grew a weeping willow tree with long, slender branches that flowed down to create a secluded canopy of leaves.

Once we sat down, Arthur rested his arm comfortably across my shoulders and we silently took in the view. Water rhythmically lapped against the bank and I spotted a few ducks paddling by.

After a few moments of silence, Arthur quietly said, "Sarah?"

"Yes?"

"Have you thought about kissing?"

I froze as still as a statue.

Up until now, Arthur and I had only shared kisses on the cheek. I knew that we would eventually get to the point in our relationship when we would kiss on the lips, but I wasn't sure if I was ready yet. Stalling for time, I decided to answer his question literally. "Um, yes, I've thought about it...have you thought about it?"

"Yes. I like kissing," he said simply. But he didn't make any moves, seeming to possess all the patience in the world. The ball was in my court.

Oh great.

Part of me wished that I could just kiss a guy without overthinking things, but it wasn't that simple for me. If I kissed Arthur, that would indicate that I was interested in progressing with our relationship. And yet, I wasn't head over heels in love with him yet. Furthermore, kissing would make it harder if we ever ended things between us.

On the other hand, the time seemed ripe to start testing the waters of attraction between us. Maybe the fireworks would finally explode as our lips met! That's what happened in the movies, right?

I glanced around to see if we were alone—there wasn't a soul in sight. A gentle breeze fluttered through my hair, and I realized that I may never encounter a more perfect opportunity.

I finally turned toward Arthur. "I think we should just *practice* kissing, because I don't know how."

"I'd be happy to help you practice." Arthur studied my face as if observing a fine work of art, then dropped his gaze to my lips.

I held my breath and closed my eyes.

His lips, ever so softly, met mine.

I waited for the fireworks but didn't feel a thing. Perplexed, I opened my eyes. *Maybe we didn't do it right.*

"Wow!" Arthur flashed me a lovey-dovey grin. "Want to practice again?"

I nodded.

Arthur leaned in again with more passion. This time I also pressed in harder, as if trying to squeeze some emotion out of the kiss. But still, nothing. I flopped back against the bench, deflated.

Arthur, on the other hand, seemed to be floating up to the clouds. "It's so wonderful to share this moment with you," he said sweetly.

Oh great, now he's even more in love with me than before!

"I'm looking forward to our premarital class next week," Arthur commented.

My shoulder blades tightened. "So soon?"

"I don't want you to feel any obligation. This class will be a good opportunity to learn about relationships." He reached down to squeeze my hand. "It will be helpful, no matter who you end up marrying."

While I appreciated Arthur's attempt to put me at ease, I could tell that his heart was on the line, vulnerable and open. I just wasn't sure if I could offer mine in return. There was so much that I still didn't understand about love. Hopefully, this class would help me figure out if we were truly meant to be together. Or not.

TWELVE
HOMEWORK

Homework?! After the first session of the premarital class, we were actually assigned homework. The class itself was fine, we mainly just did introductions, but the homework stumped me. I guess I was getting a taste of my own medicine.

During my lunch break, I fidgeted with my pen and stared at the sheet of questions: "What is the purpose of marriage? Why do you want to potentially marry your boyfriend/girlfriend?"

I don't even know if I want to marry Arthur! Maybe I should back out now.

Hearing my tummy rumble, I pushed aside the paper and dashed to the staff lounge to retrieve my lunch from the fridge. I was about to return to my classroom, when I spotted my bespectacled colleague, Dr. Mandran, eating lunch alone at one of the tables.

An idea suddenly popped into my head. Maybe I could get some advice from the smartest man on campus.

In addition to his advanced science degrees, he had been married for many years. He was certainly qualified to speak on the topic of love.

"Hey, Dr. Mandran." I plopped down my lunch bag and took a seat across from him. "How're your classes going?"

He carefully wiped his mouth with a napkin before speaking. "They're going well, thank you. We're cramming for the A.P. exams coming up."

"Can I ask you a question? It's not school-related or anything."

"Of course! What's up?"

"Well, I'm dating this guy, Arthur. Maybe you saw him at prom? Anyway, he seems really interested in me." I fiddled with the zipper on my lunch bag. "But I don't know how I feel about him. So I'm wondering, how did you make the decision to get married?"

"Ah, I remember it well." Dr. Mandran leaned back in his chair with stars in his eyes. "I was a college student, and one day, while I was riding the bus, I saw this beautiful woman. I asked her out and we started dating. Eventually, we got married."

"But *why* did you decide to get married?"

"Because we were head over heels in love! That's why!" Dr. Mandran smiled broadly as if he had just fallen in love yesterday, instead of decades ago.

"Hmm." This wasn't the logic-based reasoning I was expecting. Was being "head over heels in love" the only reason to get married?

Dr. Mandran's next words surprised me. "I think I met Arthur before. His last name is Tham, right?"

"Yes, but how on earth do you know my boyfriend?"

"I met him when he was volunteering for a political campaign," Dr. Mandran explained. "He and a group of volunteers were working to pass Proposition 35 to combat human trafficking."

"Wow! He never mentioned that."

"It really was awesome!" Dr. Mandran's eyes lit up passionately. "Did you know they got that proposition passed with the highest voter approval in California history? I can't believe you're dating Arthur. He's really a great guy."

I hadn't known that Arthur had a passion for fighting human trafficking or that he had been involved in such a historic campaign. But before I could ask any follow up questions, the door swung open and Pastor Lee strolled by. He was a frequent visitor on campus and we often chatted together about how to support my international students.

"Hey, Pastor Lee, do you have a minute?" I was curious if a scientist or a pastor would have a better under-standing of love.

"Sure, what's going on?"

"I've been talking to Dr. Mandran about my boyfriend, Arthur Tham, and I'm trying to figure out—"

"Wait, I know Arthur!" Pastor Lee exclaimed.

"You do?"

"Yeah! We volunteer together a lot. He's the commu-nity service liaison at his church. He helps organize projects, and he encourages people from his church to get involved."

"Really?" A light flipped on in my mind. So this was how Arthur had been using part of his sabbatical—by serving.

"During Christmas, he helped collect dozens of gifts for needy children," Pastor Lee continued. "He's got a big heart! I'm so glad to hear that you guys are dating. Did you say you had a question?"

"No, not really. Not anymore."

I shook my head in disbelief at what had just occurred. What were the odds that these two men knew Arthur? Somehow, it seemed like the universe was conspiring to bring us together. Or was it God? This yet again confirmed what I already knew deep in my soul—Arthur possessed the qualities that would matter in the long run.

But as I headed back to my classroom, I still couldn't help but wonder, was Arthur's sterling character and 5-star reviews enough to make up for the lack of chemistry?

I POPPED a crunchy french fry into my mouth as I sat across from Arthur in a fast- food booth. We were on our way to our next premarital class and had stopped for a quick bite to eat. It was a humid evening, and even though I was dressed in a sleeveless blouse and flowy skirt, I was still grateful for the air conditioning. Arthur wore a short-sleeve blue polo shirt which showed off his tanned arms.

"Would you like to review my homework?" Arthur

pulled out a neatly typed sheet of paper from his bag. "You can pull out your red pen and fix all the typos!"

I giggled. "No, I won't do that. But seriously, I would love to see what you wrote." I relocated to his side of the booth, so we could sit shoulder to shoulder.

Arthur read aloud, "What is the purpose of marriage? Marriage is starting a new family with a friend to share life, have children, and grow in relationship with God together."

"Wow, that's a well-thought-out answer. I really like how you described marriage as starting a new family with a friend."

"Hope I get a good grade for that!"

"Definitely!"

"Ok, next question," Arthur continued to read. "Why do you want to potentially marry your boyfriend/girlfriend?"

My ears perked up.

"I am in a relationship that could lead to marriage with Sarah because she is an amazing woman. We have similar values and are heading in the same direction in life. I admire her love for Jesus, kindness, intelligence, and beauty."

I was struck speechless. Arthur's words touched a deep part of my heart. To hear how he truly felt about me made me want to both burst with joy and burst into tears. His words of affirmation felt like a faucet pouring love into my bucket. All I could do was whisper, "That means a lot to me."

Arthur set down his paper and wrapped his arm

around me. I could feel the strength of his muscles against my body, yet as he began to gently skim up and down my bare arm, his touch was as light as a feather. I slid closer, as if I were being pulled by a magnet, until my head was resting on his shoulder, and I breathed in his intoxicating, cinnamon scent.

"I'd love to hear what you wrote, too," Arthur said in a low voice.

I picked up my homework sheet and attempted to read, but I couldn't concentrate at all. *That's strange.* I could always concentrate on reading, even with noisy students in a room. "Maybe later," I murmured as I set down my paper.

Arthur wove his fingers through my thick hair and then brushed it to the side. Slowly, he caressed back and forth across my neck and shoulders, sending delicious tingles down my spine. Heat filled my body, but it wasn't just from the humidity. I closed my eyes and savored the feel of his skin on mine. I didn't want him to ever stop. Ever.

Hope soared to the clouds like a rocket. Maybe kissing didn't move the needle for me yet, but kind words and sweet cuddles certainly did! We just had to experiment with different types of affection to see what lit my fire.

Yet, as wonderful as it was to experience romantic love, I knew that infatuation would eventually ebb and flow. We would need both the sparks of chemistry and the steadiness of character to carry us forward.

My flushed face beamed up at Arthur. "I love all this touching, but we better get to our class before we're tardy!"

THIRTEEN

WELL-SUITED

"Ready to help me pick out an interview suit?" Arthur opened the passenger door of his car for me, and I slid inside. It was a cloudless, carefree Saturday in early May, the kind of day you dream about during the dead of winter. Summer break was right around the corner and change was in the air—in the weather, in Arthur, and in me—although I couldn't fully put my finger on it.

"I'm not an expert on men's fashion, but I'll try my best." I smoothed out my white sundress which hit above my knees and actually let my legs see the light of day for once. As my confidence rose higher, so did my hemlines, and Arthur didn't seem to mind one bit.

As he climbed into his side of the car, he commented, "You look beautiful in that dress!" He leaned closer and landed a soft kiss on my lips. "Of course, you look beautiful every day."

I savored his warm lips on mine. My appetite for affection was growing the more I got a taste of its sweetness, and Arthur was more than happy to introduce me to all of its varieties.

As we drove to the mall, Arthur caught me up on the latest developments. "A few days ago, a recruiter called me out of the blue about a marketing analyst job."

"That sounds promising."

"Yeah, I'm excited about it. This sabbatical has been fun, but I'm eager to get back into the workforce. Especially since things are getting more serious with us."

Serious. I glanced out the window and pondered Arthur's word choice.

Our premarital class had flown by, and over the past few weeks, we had dug into the nitty-gritty topics such as children, work, and household responsibilities. Time and time again, I had found myself surprised at how remarkably aligned we were in our opinions, as if we were cut from the same cloth. While I hadn't completely made up my mind yet if I wanted to marry Arthur, I was definitely considering it as a possibility for the future. The distant future. No need to get serious yet.

We arrived at the large department store and found our way to the men's department. Shiny metal racks greeted us with an impressive array of suits, dress shirts, and neckties. My shoulders relaxed and I slowed my pace to take it all in. The atmosphere of orderliness calmed me —everything was neatly arranged by size, color, and style. I wished that my entire life could be as neat and tidy as this store. But life, especially life with Arthur, was proving to be unpredictable.

"What color suit do you think I should get?" Arthur's question brought me back to the task at hand.

"You already have a black suit that you wore to prom. So how about a steel gray color?" I combed through the first rack until I spotted a suit that matched my description and lifted it up for Arthur to see.

He ran his hands down the fabric and inspected the buttons, pockets, and inner lining. "Looks good to me." He draped the suit jacket and matching pants over his arm and we moved on to look at dress shirts.

As we continued to browse, I finally gathered the courage to ask the question that had been nagging me. "You mentioned that you really want this job since we're getting more serious. But I'm wondering, don't you have some concerns about me before getting too serious? We just met a few months ago."

Arthur selected a white dress shirt and then replied, "I think we're good for each other." He paused and chewed on his lip. "But, if you want to know the truth, I do have a concern about you."

"What is it? My long work hours?"

Arthur looked earnestly into my eyes. "I'm concerned that you won't want to get married as soon as I do."

"What do you mean?" I shot him a quizzical look. "How soon do you want to get married? Hypothetically, of course."

"I'd like to get married this year."

I reached for a rack to steady myself as the room began to spin. "Are you joking?"

Arthur gave a small laugh. "I've been trying to get

married for years, but it's been hard to find the right match." He took a step forward to gently stroke my arm. "So now that I've found someone as wonderful as you, I can't wait to get started on our future together."

His desire for me was palpable, and my heart beat faster. But marriage sounded wild and unknown, just like roller coasters or haunted houses—both of which I actively avoided. I wasn't sure if I was courageous enough to take that leap yet.

"Couples usually date for a year or two before getting engaged," I pointed out. "Then they spend at least six months planning their wedding. We still have plenty of time to figure this out. What's the big rush?"

Arthur ran his hand through his hair. "You know I'm already 33, and I really hope to have kids one day. But I'm worried that if I wait too long...that might not happen."

Oh dear. I turned away and diverted my attention toward a colorful display of ties.

"I know this puts you in a tricky spot," Arthur spoke slowly. "You're still young and you haven't had much opportunity to date other men. You might not be ready to settle down yet. But I am. So that's why I'm concerned."

I sighed and handed him a silver tie. "Why don't you go try everything on? I need time to think."

"Take all the time you need. Sorry to spring this on you. I wasn't expecting to talk about this right now, right *here*."

I plopped down on a chair outside the dressing room, while Arthur tried on his items. I put my hands on my head which felt like it was about to burst like an overfilled balloon. I did want to marry Arthur. Eventually. Maybe I could just stall for time?

The dressing room door creaked open and I glanced up. Arthur strolled out in his gray suit, white dress shirt, and silver tie.

"Wow!" I rose to my feet and looked him over from top to bottom. The suit made him look even more manly, steady, and put-together than usual. He walked over to a full-length mirror, and I joined him. He drew his arm around my waist and pulled me close to his side. As I studied our reflection—him in his suit and tie, and me in my white sundress—I knew that this could be a glimpse of our future selves.

"You look great," I gently patted his chest.

"I look better when you're by my side."

I blushed. "So, I've been thinking. I would be ok if we start talking about *hypothetical* wedding timelines."

"Really?" Arthur's eyes widened and a smile exploded across his face. "That's the best news I've ever heard! What needs to happen for you to feel comfortable moving forward?"

"Hmm." I tried to think of requirements that would buy me more time. "On your side of things, you would need to get a job, of course. At some point, I would like to meet your dad. And since you and your mom live together, you would need to figure out living arrangements for the future."

"Ok." Arthur's head bobbed up and down. "That's all doable."

"And on my side, I need to get a dental surgery done over my summer break."

I figured that would buy me at least a few months of time before I had to face the actual decision of getting engaged and married.

I would be so wrong.

SUMMER

FOURTEEN
SUGAR HIGH

My groggy eyes cracked open as the morning sun shone through my bedroom blinds, and I instantly regretted being conscious. I should have stayed in dreamland longer where there was no such thing as dental surgery, gauze, or excruciating pain. I pressed my hands against my swollen, aching cheeks. *What a rotten way to kick off my summer break.*

But my mood brightened when I remembered that it was our 6-month dating anniversary. I had to get moving! I popped a pain pill, washed it down with a swig of water, then kicked off the covers. But when I stood up, the blood rushed from my head to my feet, making me lightheaded and unstable. I hadn't eaten anything solid for a few days, and it was taking a toll on my body.

Somehow, I managed to change into a white sleeveless blouse, tan skirt, and sandals. As I brushed my tangled hair and tried to make myself look half-way decent, I thought about the whirlwind of the past few weeks.

Shortly after our trip to the mall, Arthur had worn his new suit to his interview, and they practically hired him on the spot. A week after that, I found myself sitting at a Chinese dim sum restaurant meeting Arthur's dad and other relatives. And, as the grand finale, Arthur's mom jangled a new set of keys in front of us and announced that she had rented a room for herself from a nearby friend. She said that Arthur and I could have the house to ourselves if we ever decided to get married. Hint, hint.

In less than one month, Arthur had checked off all of his requirements.

I should have given him more.

And now, here I was, done with my requirement as well.

Yikes.

A FEW HOURS LATER, I turned up the air conditioning in Arthur's car to combat the summer heat coming through the windows. "Where're we going?" I mumbled while trying to move my mouth as little as possible.

"I can't tell you. It's a surprise!"

"Just a hint?"

"Well, I've been trying to figure out where to take you for lunch. I know you like bread and Mexican food, but those are out of the question since you can't chew right now."

"That's for sure."

"At first, I thought about getting ice cream. But then I thought, what's even fancier than ice cream?"

I shrugged my shoulders.

"Gelato!"

"Mmmm. Where?"

"It's at an exclusive card-carrying-members-only club."

I eyed him suspiciously.

"I'm not kidding," he protested. "Just you wait!"

A little while later, Arthur did in fact pull into the parking lot of an exclusive card-carrying-members-only club: Costco.

My hands flew to my mouth to prevent me from laughing, but it was too late. *Ouch*. Arthur's humor had gotten the better of me.

"Sorry to make you laugh," Arthur said sheepishly. "They really do have gelato. It's only at select locations."

I motioned for us to get going.

Once inside the food court, Arthur purchased our treats and we sat across from each other at a red and white table. The place was chaotic and buzzing with dozens of other customers who were chowing down on pizza slices, hot dogs, and chicken bakes.

But everything faded as I closed my eyes and took my first bite. The cold, creamy vanilla gelato danced inside my mouth and numbed my pain, while the sugar pumped fresh energy into my bloodstream.

"This is *so* good!" I reopened my eyes to find Arthur grinning at me, and I couldn't help but give a small smile back. *What a guy*. He had known exactly what would make me feel better and had catered the whole date around my needs.

"Sarah?" Arthur's gaze intensified. "I've been thinking."

"About what?"

"I want to get married to you. Unequivocally." His chocolate brown eyes shone with hopeful longing.

Is he semi-proposing? In a Costco food court? And did he just use the word "unequivocally" in a sentence? I set down my spoon and stared at him, not quite believing my ears.

When I didn't respond, he continued. "I know we've been talking about hypothetical timelines, but I'd like to really start nailing down plans. How do you feel about getting married in November? You'll have a week off for Thanksgiving break—it'll be perfect."

"But that's just five months from now!" I wildly gestured with my hands since my voice wasn't strong enough to express my shock. "I don't think we could pull it off." My mind spun with logistics. We'd have to ask my parents for their blessing, find an engagement ring, get engaged, and then plan a whole wedding.

"I think we *can* do it." Arthur's face lit up as if he were Einstein and about to reveal the greatest idea on earth. "Since you have the summer off from teaching, why not just get a head start on planning our wedding now?"

"But we're not even engaged yet."

"I know."

"You want to literally plan our wedding before getting engaged?"

MATCH MADE ONLINE   99

"Yes, it's very practical."

"But no one does that!"

"We don't have to be like everyone else."

"People will think we're crazy."

"Let them think whatever they want. Who cares? We have to figure out what's best for us."

I just stared at him. Part of me admired his guts to march to the beat of his own drum. He didn't seem constrained by tradition or other people's opinions. He certainly wouldn't end up in a cult. He was too free-thinking, too much of a maverick.

"But hey, no need to respond right now." Arthur waved his hands. "Take some time to think about it." With that, he casually took another bite of gelato.

I sat back in disbelief, utterly speechless, and not just because of my mouth pain.

As I swirled my gelato with my spoon, thoughts also swirled through my mind. *Should I agree to start planning our wedding?* This situation was forcing me to make up my mind about marriage sooner than I had anticipated. But I couldn't actually think of a good reason to *not* move forward with Arthur's proposed timeline, other than it being unconventional. We had already finished our premarital class, we had a house lined up, and our relationship was deepening every day. Furthermore, I had no doubts about Arthur and his character. Everything that I had seen these past few months revealed that he possessed a heart of gold.

This was my dream coming true—to find a wonderful

man and build a home together. So what was holding me back?

Just myself. I had spent so much of my life guarding my heart and avoiding love, so I wasn't sure if I was mature enough to be a wife. What if I made a mess of everything?

But something about Arthur's confidence encouraged me. He seemed to believe that I was ready for marriage. He seemed to believe that we were a great match. For now, I could borrow some of his confidence until I could find my own.

"Ok." I took a deep breath. "Let's start planning our wedding!"

FIFTEEN
DIAMONDS

The glass display case felt cool beneath my hands as I peered inside at the sparkling diamond rings.

"See anything you like?" Arthur stood behind me and slid his arms around my waist.

"Nah, not yet." I sighed. "But let's keep looking around."

Over the past few weeks we had visited countless jewelry stores, searching for the perfect engagement ring. I had been told to not settle for anything less than my dream ring. After all, you only get engaged once, hopefully. I envisioned a round solitaire diamond set in a silver-colored band. Specifically, I had my heart set on finding a band that looked like two strands twisted together, to represent our connected lives. However, this style was nowhere to be found.

Arthur leaned against a display case to face me. "By the way, I had a great lunch with your parents the other day."

"And?" I held my breath.

"And they formally gave their blessing for us to get married!"

"Yay, that's great news!" I clapped my hands together.

"Your mom even cried happy tears—it was really touching. It's obvious how much your parents love you."

"It's a big deal for them, since I'm the first of my siblings to move toward marriage. You know they've always been very protective of us." I wrapped my arms around my body as I thought about their comforting security.

"You're going to blaze the trail for your other siblings. By the time Rebekah wants to get married, your parents will probably be eager to have an empty nest." Arthur chuckled.

"I've been making lots of progress with our wedding planning. I called my church secretary to reserve the church for our wedding, and she nearly fainted with excitement. She didn't even know that I was dating."

"I'm sure you're raising lots of eyebrows!" Arthur grinned.

"Oh, and I just bought my wedding dress!" I chattered like an excited squirrel. "And your mom took me to Chinatown to buy a traditional qipao dress for me to wear at the reception. And speaking of reception, I'm over-the-moon excited that we're going to have it at a Mexican restaurant! It's going to be so fun to blend our cultures together."

"Wow, you've done a lot in a short amount of time!"

"Well, I do love to plan. And you're right, this summer

break is the perfect opportunity since I have more time and energy than I usually do during the school year."

"I've been getting a lot done, too." Arthur whipped out his phone to show me some websites. "I set up our wedding registry account and I also created a spreadsheet to track our guest list and their RSVPs. But of course, we can't send out our invitations until after we're engaged."

"Which is why we must find a ring!" I declared. With renewed motivation, we returned to the search.

Arthur scanned a display case and then pointed to a particular ring. "Is that what you're looking for?"

I leaned in closer to inspect it. "Not quite. That band does have a little twist, but I want two strands that are intertwined. It has to be just right."

"Ok, got it," Arthur replied, but his puzzled face told me otherwise. "How about we go ask someone for help?"

Susan, the nearest salesperson, introduced herself and then set off to search the store, high and low, for a ring that matched my description. She returned empty-handed. "Sorry, I don't think we have anything like that." Scratching her head, she suddenly remembered something. "Well, there's one more place I can check." She dashed off to the back room.

I slumped into a chair and waited.

"Don't worry." Arthur put his arm around my shoulders. "If this doesn't work out, we can keep looking at other stores."

"It just feels awkward doing all this wedding planning without being engaged yet. My friends seem...concerned. Of course, Zia is all for it. But everyone else keeps asking why I'm planning my wedding before getting engaged." I recalled how one friend had even laughed out loud because she thought I was joking around.

"I can't wait to get engaged either. I'd do it today if I could." As if to prove the sincerity of his words, Arthur leaned in to give me a slow kiss.

In a few minutes, Susan returned with a velvet-lined tray.

I rose to my feet.

And staring up at me was my dream ring! The band was made of polished white gold with two strands wrapped around each other like a rope, while a large, round diamond sparkled from the center.

"That's it! That's my ring!" I could hardly believe my eyes.

"Would you like to try it on?" she asked.

I picked up the delicate ring and slipped it on my finger. The diamond caught the light and reflected rainbows as I slowly turned my hand from side to side. I had never seen anything so beautiful.

"So *this* is what you've been talking about." Arthur wiped his forehead in relief.

"We can finally get engaged!" I squealed and floated up into the clouds.

Perceiving my enthusiasm, Susan wasted no time ringing up the transaction. As she entered our information into the computer, she off-handedly asked, "You don't have allergies to any metals, do you?"

"Wait, what?" Her question brought me back down to

earth with a thud. "Actually, I do. I'm allergic to nickel. It makes me itchy."

Susan looked through her glasses and studied the ring. "This is made of white gold and it may contain a small amount of nickel."

"Oh no!" My heart froze. "What can we do?"

"To be safe, we can order a custom ring made from platinum which is naturally nickel-free. It will look identical. However, it will take several weeks since it's a custom order."

"Several weeks?" Arthur furrowed his brow. "When will it be ready?"

Susan clicked around on her computer, then reported, "The middle of September, hopefully."

I shook my head, not wanting to believe my ears. That would be only two months before our wedding!

Arthur gestured towards me. "It's up to you, Sarah. We can wait for this one or try to find another ring that could be ready sooner."

My eyes shifted back and forth between the ring and Arthur. Even though it would delay our engagement, there was no way that I could pass up this ring. "Let's go ahead and order it."

Unfortunately, this situation left us in the fragile and uncertain zone of not-quite-engaged.

SIXTEEN
HARDBALL

Peanut shells crunched beneath our tennis shoes as Arthur and I mounted the concrete steps that led to our bleacher seats. An afternoon baseball game in the warm July sunshine was just the break we needed from all the wedding planning. I breathed in the smell of freshly cut grass and took in the vast sea of eager fans. I finally spotted my dad's best friend, decked out in a jersey and cap, and we slid into the seats next to him.

"Hi Mr. Lin! Long time no see!" I gave him a friendly hug. "I'd like to introduce you to my boyfriend, Arthur."

"Glad to finally meet you." Mr. Lin extended his hand. "Sarah's dad has told me so much about you."

"Thanks for inviting us," Arthur replied with a firm handshake.

Mr. Lin and my dad were best friends, and his kids and I grew up together, so he was like an uncle to me. Nevertheless, I hadn't seen him in years, so I was surprised when he reached out and sent me two tickets to join him for a baseball game.

Crack! The sound of the ball hitting the bat drew my attention to the field, and for the first few innings, I got swept up in the energy of the crowd and the fierce competition between the teams. Arthur and I shared a pepperoni pizza from a cardboard box and we made small talk with Mr. Lin who knew everything about baseball and was more than happy to explain the latest stats to us.

As the hours ticked by, the sky grew darker, and the stadium lights flipped on. During the seventh inning stretch, Mr. Lin cleared his throat and turned to face me. "So, Sarah, I heard that you met Arthur on an online dating site. I didn't even know you were interested in dating." His friendly tone was gone and he was suddenly all business.

"I just started dating last year and Arthur's the second guy I met. I guess I got lucky." I offered a small smile which wasn't returned.

"How long ago did you meet?"

"About 7 months ago."

"That's not much time at all. And your dad told me that you're already planning your wedding! Is that true?"

"Yes, that's right." I shifted in my seat, which had suddenly become hard and uncomfortable.

"I don't see a ring." Mr. Lin drew his eyebrows together. "Why are you planning a wedding when you're not engaged yet? That doesn't make any sense."

My eyes dropped to my bare left ring finger. "We ordered a ring, but it won't be here until September.

While we're waiting, we're getting a head start on planning since our wedding is coming up in November."

"*This* November?" Mr. Lin dramatically clutched his chest as if I were giving him a heart attack.

"Yes." Sweat began to bead on my forehead.

"This isn't like you at all! I've always known you to be a cautious girl. Don't you think you're rushing?"

My mouth went dry.

Seeing my distress, Arthur leaned forward and inserted himself into the conversation. "Sure, it's a little quicker than typical. But we've already done premarital counseling, we've taken the time to meet each other's families and friends, and—"

"You should date at least a year before getting engaged," Mr. Lin interrupted. "Maybe two or three years. Everyone knows that."

"That might be true for other people, but each couple has a different situation. We know we are a good match, so why wait?" Arthur tried to keep his tone light. "Besides, I'm not getting any younger."

"How old are you, anyway?"

"I'm 33."

"Sheesh! That's quite older than Sarah. Why are you robbing the cradle?" Mr. Lin laughed, but his eyes were icy.

I watched Arthur's face turn red. His hand gripped the plastic armrest, and he pursed his lips together as if holding back some choice words.

Mr. Lin didn't back down. "Sarah, you're still young. You should date more people before settling down. Don't let this guy rush you before you've had time to play the field. You're not ready to get married. I think you're making a big mistake."

All around me, I could hear the crowd chanting, but all of that was irrelevant to the spectacle that was unfolding right in front of me.

Mr. Lin was unearthing all of the doubts that I had tried to keep under wraps over the past few weeks. I couldn't make sense of my scrambled emotions, so I chose the next best option: run away. "Thank you for your concern. It's getting late. We need to leave now to beat the crowds before the game ends." I rose from my seat on wobbly legs and motioned Arthur to follow me.

Mr. Lin called out after us, "I'll see you at your wedding. *Next* November."

Darkness and silence enveloped us as we drove back to my home. We didn't even tune into the radio to find out who had won the baseball game.

Once we arrived at my house, Arthur walked me to my front door, and we paused under the glowing porch light.

"I'm so sorry about what happened back there." I wrapped my arms around his waist and pressed my face into his chest. "I wasn't expecting that at all."

"I kind of felt like I was being fed to the lions at the Roman Colosseum." Arthur exhaled a deep breath, as if he had been holding it for the past hour. "I don't agree with Mr. Lin, but I know he's well-meaning. Everyone is enti-tled to their own opinions. The important thing is that we are confident in our own decision, right?" With that, he lifted my chin to kiss me goodnight, then disappeared into the moonlight shadows.

I wished that I shared the unshakable confidence that Arthur possessed, but tonight had left me rattled and questioning everything. *Am I really prepared for marriage?* I would have to figure this out tomorrow. For now, all I wanted was to disappear under a pile of blankets until morning. However, when I opened the front door, I found my parents waiting for me on the couch.

Uh oh.

"Sarah, come sit with us for a little bit," my mom gestured to the chair facing them.

I hesitantly lowered myself down. A chill ran down my spine as I analyzed their serious faces.

My dad spoke first. "As you've probably heard, we've been talking to Mr. Lin these past few weeks. We actually just got off the phone with him."

"What did he say?"

My dad sighed. "He's really worried that you're rushing headlong into marriage. And we agree with him. We have nothing against Arthur, he's a great guy. We're just concerned about you."

"What?"

My mom's forehead creased with worry, the same way she used to look at me when I was a child with a splinter in my finger. "We're so sorry, we've changed our mind. We don't want you to get married this November. You need to postpone."

SEVENTEEN
CRUSHED

"The wedding is off," I choked out the words into my cell phone as I sat cross-legged on my bed. "I just spoke to my parents and they...they changed their mind." I pulled a blanket around my shaking body, but no blanket in the world was warm enough to melt the ice that had frozen my very core.

"What? No!" Arthur's voice crackled with tension. "Why?"

"They want us to spend more time getting to know each other."

"I can't believe this. Just a couple of weeks ago they gave us their blessing! So, what does this mean?"

"My parents want us to wait another year."

"Another year?" Arthur sounded incredulous.

"Another year *at the minimum*." I let out a sigh. "And my parents and Mr. Lin aren't the only ones concerned. Lots of people think we're rushing. Maybe they're right...."

"I was afraid this might happen." Arthur sighed. "I knew it was a risk to date you. You're young, and I'm your first boyfriend. And you're the first of your siblings wanting to get married, so of course people are protective of you. But on my side, all my friends and family are thrilled to see me move toward marriage."

"I just feel confused about everything now." I swallowed a lump in my throat as tears stung my eyes. "Maybe I'm not even ready to get married!"

Arthur let out a long breath. "Look, I don't want to pressure you to do anything you don't want to do. You are free to walk away. Or we can get married later. But please don't string me along and postpone getting married indefinitely."

"What do you mean?"

"What if we wait another year, and then you decide to break up after that? You would have no problem finding another guy. But that would put me in a tough spot. I'd have to start all over with dating. The older I get, the harder it is for me to get married and have kids. So if you honestly don't intend to marry me, please let me know sooner than later."

"Even if I wanted to get married in November, I can't go against my parents!" I protested.

Arthur spoke slowly, with conviction. "Sarah, your parents can have their opinion, but remember that the ultimate decision is up to you. It's not even up to me. You already know that I want to marry you. But the final decision is yours and yours alone."

My jaw dropped. I had fully expected Arthur to throw up his hands in defeat and join me in my pity party, but no, here he was, challenging me to think for myself.

"Let's take a break from wedding planning." Arthur seemed ready to wrap up our call. "Take some time to decide what you want to do."

"I will."

"And Sarah? Please let it be your final decision. I don't think I could take it if you changed your mind again after that. I need to know how you really feel." His voice, which had been strong and steady, cracked with fragility.

"Ok."

"Goodnight," Arthur said softly and hung up.

I tossed my phone onto my bedside table with a *thud* and covered my face with my hands. My dream of marriage was beginning to fade. I was tempted to just jump off this dating roller coaster and return to the familiarity of my old, single life. If only I could be like Peter Pan and never grow up, or like Simba and live the "hakuna matata" life.

But what about Arthur? The thought of setting him free to fly away and build a nest with someone else made my heart ache with regret. But it felt like the fairest thing to do. Sure, I could ask him to wait longer for me, but there were no guarantees that my parents wouldn't change their mind again. No guarantees that I wouldn't succumb to self-doubt and change *my* mind.

As if right on cue, my bedroom door burst open and Fear slithered in.

He had grown to mammoth proportions since my previous encounter with him. Like an exotic dancer, he seductively twisted and teased his way around my feet and legs, leaving me paralyzed on my bed.

Looping his powerful coils, he spiraled higher to pin my arms against my torso.

Rough scales rubbed against my skin.

He was now up to my neck.

Without warning, he tightened his solid body and a tingly sensation coursed through my body.

I was losing circulation.

I found myself staring into his mesmerizing eyes. His jet-black pupils looked like slits.

His forked tongue flicked from side to side as he hissed, "This is the perfect chance to get out of this relationship! You're too timid and naive. You don't know how to be a good wife anyway. You'll make a mess of marriage and everything will go down in flames."

He began to squeeze harder, cutting off my blood flow. Within minutes, I knew my heart would cease to function and he would devour me.

I frantically scanned the room, looking for an escape, and my eyes landed on the Bible that sat on my bedside table. A memory from over a decade earlier flashed through my mind.

Right after my family had left the Institute, I had been tossed around, anchorless and uncertain of what I believed. I didn't know which rules I had to follow in order to still be good enough for God. I vividly remembered one sleepless night, when I picked up my Bible and began reading it for myself. In the dim light, I flipped through the pages, until I came across Ephesians 2:8–9. "For it is by grace you have been saved, through faith—and this is not from yourselves, it is the gift of God—not by works, so that no one can boast."

This message was contrary to what I had been taught —that I had to work hard to gain God's favor. Yet this verse presented a different way. A way of grace. Salvation was a free gift, not something that I had to earn. That night, tears of relief and gratitude rolled down my cheeks as I fully put my faith in Jesus and His goodness, instead of in my own.

Hiss! Fear's pointed snout came into view, bringing my attention back to my current crisis. Suddenly, a revelation struck me. Grace was the answer. Just as I had been saved by grace, I could continue relying on God's grace.

Fear had been telling me only half of the story.

Yes, Fear was right, I was timid and naive and I didn't have all the skills to be a perfect wife. But by God's grace, I could learn and grow. I already had grown so much this past year.

Yes, Fear was right, I would make mistakes in marriage. But God's grace would cover all of that. And Arthur would show me grace, too. He already had in so many ways. He loved me and I loved him. And our roots would grow down into God's love and keep us strong. So why wait any longer to get married?

In one final attempt to destroy me, Fear compressed my entire body in his deadly embrace. With gasping breaths, I cried out to God, "I do want to get married. To Arthur. In November. Please help me!"

And He heard me.

My gracious Savior swept down, and in one swift motion, crushed the head of Fear.

I was finally free.

AUTUMN

EIGHTEEN
AT LAST

"Well, well, well. Look who's finally getting married!" Zia announced as she breezed into the church bridal room dressed in a tan sweater dress and tall, brown boots.

"What do you mean, *finally*?" I rose from my chair where my hair was being styled and planted my hands on my hips with playful indignation. "It was only 11 months ago that Arthur and I had our first date!"

"I'm glad you hung in there. Lord knows how many times you almost got scared off!" She patted my shoulder as if to make sure that I wasn't a figment of her imagination. "I'm here as your official support person to make sure you don't get cold feet. I better lock these doors just in case you try to bolt." Her infectious laugh filled the room like warm sunshine, and I couldn't help but join in.

"Don't worry, I'm not going anywhere! This is right where I'm supposed to be."

Zia lowered her voice, "Did you ever work things out with your parents?"

"Yes, thank goodness. Arthur and I talked through all their concerns, and they eventually came around. I think the whole situation, as stressful as it was, helped my parents to finally view me as a grown woman who's capable of making her own decisions."

"That's right! Now you're talking!"

"And it also grew my faith in God. I realized that I don't have to be so afraid of marriage because God will help both me and Arthur with whatever we face." I raised my arms as if I were a bird stretching her wings. "I feel so light and free, like a burden has been lifted off my shoulders."

"That's wonderful to hear!"

"Thank you for all your support. I wouldn't be here today if it wasn't for you."

"I've always got your back!" Zia drew me into a warm embrace and let out a sniffle. "Ok, I'll let you get back to your beauty treatments, but call me if you need anything."

Filled with anticipation, I could barely sit still as my hairstylist finished curling my hair. Half my hair was swept up and secured with a silver clip, while the rest of my hair flowed down my back like a waterfall. Next, my makeup artist unzipped her black cases and worked her magic with blush, mascara, and lipstick to transform me into a bride.

A sparkle caught the sunlight, and I glanced down at my left hand to admire my engagement ring. Engagement ring 2.0. Turns out, the order for our first engagement ring couldn't be fulfilled after all. So in the interest of time, I had selected a new style which could be ready much sooner. After all, it was just a ring—the love we shared was the real treasure.

Ever the romantic, Arthur had taken me back to the charming white gazebo at Woodland Park and gotten down on one knee and proposed.

I said yes, of course.

I looked up from my ring to see my mom and sisters buzzing around me like bees for the final preparations. They zipped, fluffed, and adjusted my white gown which was covered in delicate lace patterns. Then they slipped on my accessories—a sparkly necklace, a silver bracelet, and drop earrings with white pearls on the bottom. A hush fell over the room as my mom pinned the elegant, sheer veil onto the back of my hair and smoothed it with her hands.

"My little girl is all grown up," she declared with watery eyes. "I'm so happy for you."

I wrapped my arms around her, thankful for the loving cocoon which she had tried her best to provide for me.

But now it was time for me to burst forth on my own.

A few minutes later, my sisters and I giggled and chatted as we lined up outside the church, waiting for our cue to enter. They wore knee-length turquoise dresses and clutched bright yellow bouquets. The morning air was deliciously crisp and arching above us was a brilliant blue sky, the kind of day that only comes in November. Even the trees seemed to know it was a festive occasion as they dressed themselves in fiery red, orange, and yellow leaves.

The processional music began and my sisters began their walk down the aisle.

"Are you ready?" My dad offered me his arm, looking sharp in his new suit and freshly shined shoes.

"Absolutely! Are you?"

"I'm going to miss having you around all the time." He cleared a frog out of his throat. "But I'm so glad that you and Arthur found each other."

"Me, too."

With that, we stepped through the door, crossing the threshold that separated my past from my future.

As we slowly made our way down the aisle, a solo pianist played an emotional, uplifting melody that reminded me of being on top of a mountain with wind blowing through my hair. Sunshine streamed in from the large windows, illuminating the sanctuary with golden light. And everywhere I looked I saw the radiant faces of friends and family who were bursting with palpable joy— each one had played a part in our story.

I saw Zia, who had urged me to keep trying online dating.

I saw Arthur's parents, gray-haired and smiling, who had waited years for their only son to get married.

I saw Mr. Lin, who had cautioned me from marrying too quickly, but still showed up to offer support.

I saw Arthur's groomsmen, standing as proud witnesses to this special occasion.

And at the front of the church, wearing the same gray suit that we had picked out together, I saw my soon-to-be-husband. As I drew closer, I noticed his eyes were wide, as if in shock. To think of how long he had waited for this day to arrive. How long he had waited for me.

The pastor welcomed everyone with a booming voice. "Today is truly a day of answered prayers and dreams coming true!" He went on to give a simple message about marriage that was peppered with humor.

After exchanging our wedding bands, the pastor guided me and Arthur to say our vows. With voices sure and steady, we repeated each phrase as we gazed into each other's eyes. "I promise to love, honor, and be faithful to you physically, emotionally, and spiritually. May this ring be a constant reminder that I will keep the promises that I have made before God and these witnesses. I commit to love you today and always."

I took great comfort in knowing that even when life got tough, we could rely on God to help us keep our vows. He would be our firm foundation.

The rest of the ceremony flew by, and at the end of it, the pastor announced, "By the authority given to me as a minister of Jesus Christ, I now pronounce you husband and wife! Arthur, you may kiss your bride."

I felt the same exuberant thrill that I got when the school bell rang to signal the start of summer break, only this was 100 times more exciting!

I eagerly leaned in and Arthur's lips met mine. His hands encircled my waist and he gently pulled me closer to himself. His kiss was sweet like honey with a hint of spicy passion. Warmth filled my body from head to toe, and I closed my eyes to savor every sensation of that one perfect moment. We were finally united together.

All around us, the room exploded with applause. The pastor raised his voice above the noise to announce,

"Ladies and gentlemen, I have the honor to present to you, for the very first time, Mr. and Mrs. Arthur and Sarah Tham!"

Arm in arm, we bounded down the aisle. When we reached the end, Arthur drew me into his arms. "I love you, Sarah. I've been waiting forever to say that to you."

"I love you, too," I answered back. "Even though your ideas are a little crazy."

"Oh, I have more!" Arthur said with a gleam in his eye.

As I thought about the past year, I was filled with gratitude. Although we were matched online by a brilliant algorithm, I knew that God had a lot to do with bringing us together. He certainly helped us stay together and He gave me the courage to open my heart to love.

AUTHOR'S NOTE

This book was based on my own love story. When I was younger, I expected to have a simple, predictable path towards marriage. So I was quite surprised when my actual experience was filled with uncertainty, fear, and unexpected twists. I wondered, am I the only one who is anxious about dating? Am I the only one who is scared of marriage? It took a lot of courage to open my heart to love.

I have come to realize that everyone's story is complex. Our past experiences affect us deeply, and sometimes we need to conquer fear and transform our thinking in order to move forward. Even still, not all stories end happily-ever-after. But no matter what, I believe that God can use all the pieces of our lives for good.

Thank you so much for reading *Match Made Online*. I hope you enjoyed it! Reviews are very helpful for independent authors, and I would appreciate it if you left a review to let me know your thoughts.

ACKNOWLEDGMENTS

I am deeply grateful to the numerous people who have enriched both my life and the creation of this book.

I'd like to begin by thanking Arthur, my husband. I'm so glad we took a chance on each other. You are a treasure, and I appreciate you being by my side through the highs and lows of this project. Proverbs 18:22.

To my beloved daughters, Kalani and Alana, thank you for infusing my life with your boundless joy and imagination!

Big thanks to my parents for their enduring love, prayers, and support, which serve as a testament to God's grace.

I would like to offer appreciation to Laura, my wonderful mother-in-law, for welcoming me with open arms.

To my siblings, Bryan, Sam, Grace, and Rebekah—thank you for always being there for me. Special thanks to Rebekah, for spending many months shaping this book and taking it to the next level!

To Liwen, thank you for generously offering your expertise to help me edit, format, and publish this book. As a fan of your books and writing, this is a dream come true for me!

To Liane, I am so grateful for your friendship, uplifting text messages, and all your encouragement with my writing.

To Azea, thank you for nudging me to continue with online dating, and for all the ways that you have poured into my life.

Thank you to my dear friends who have been a constant source of inspiration—Jeffra, Amelia, Becca, Katie, Mary, Beka, Cassie, Lindsey, Katina, and many others.

Above all, I would like to thank God, for giving me life and breath and stories to tell.

ABOUT THE AUTHOR

Sarah Tham is a writer based in California, USA. She weaves together entertaining storylines and relatable characters, with a sprinkle of faith and humor.

She has a M.A. in Education and is a former English teacher. She loves striking up conversations with both friends and strangers, and discovering the unique stories that each life has to offer. She also enjoys spending time with her husband and two daughters.

Made in United States
Troutdale, OR
06/15/2024

20559335R20077